MORE PRECIOUS THAN DIAMONDS

Louise Gresham moved to Whitchurch, Kent almost three months ago following a painful break-up with her fiancé. Good fortune landed her a job at Whitchurch Museum, and it is here she meets handsome thirtysomething Nathaniel Prentice. After assisting Nathaniel with his lectures and accompanying him on visits to see his niece, Louise realises she is developing feelings for him. But the past has made her cautious — should she jump straight into another relationship so soon after getting her heart broken?

JEAN M. LONG

MORE PRECIOUS THAN DIAMONDS

Complete and Unabridged

LINFORD
Leicester

First published in Great Britain in 2018

First Linford Edition
published 2019

A catalogue record for this book is available
from the British Library.

ISBN 978–1–4448–4133–6

Published by
F. A. Thorpe (Publishing)
Anstey, Leicestershire

Set by Words & Graphics Ltd.
Anstey, Leicestershire
Printed and bound in Great Britain by
T. J. International Ltd., Padstow, Cornwall

This book is printed on acid-free paper

1

Locking her car, Louise hurried in the direction of the Whitchurch Museum. The sight of a red jaguar parked in Philip Dakar's personal slot, brought her to an abrupt halt. Suddenly the door opened and a youngish man unfurled himself from the driver's seat. He was very good-looking and exceptionally well-dressed, but this escaped Louise's notice as she confronted him.

'These spaces are reserved for museum personnel,' she told him firmly, pointing to the sign on the wall.

A pair of dark brown eyes surveyed her coolly. He nodded, but obviously had no intention of moving his car. Fuming at his arrogance, Louise marched off, aware that he was shouting something after her. Simultaneously, a car alarm went off drowning out his words. Glancing over her shoulder, she saw he was briskly making his way towards her, waving his arms.

Keen to avoid a further confrontation, she dodged between two cars and dived into a passageway until he'd gone past.

After a few moments, she made her way to the front entrance of the museum. Pushing open the heavy oak door, she stopped in her tracks, for there in the entrance hall, deep in conversation with Ryan Clarke, the Collections Manager, was the very person she had been trying to avoid. She stood stock still. Suddenly Ryan spotted her.

'Oh, good, Louise. You're back.'

'This man has been following me!' Louise burst out, giving the man a fierce glare.

Her pursuer appeared taken aback whilst Ryan looked distinctly uncomfortable. 'You've obviously completely misconstrued the situation, Louise. Mr Prentice tried to catch up with you because you dropped these!'

Ryan dangled her car keys in front of her.

Louise who had been convinced that the stranger was up to no good, subsided onto the nearest chair — muttering her apologies and feeling foolish. Fortunately, apart from themselves and a steward at the far end, the area was deserted.

To Louise's relief, she saw that Mr Prentice, whoever he was, now looked amused. He crossed to Louise's side and extended a hand. 'Nathaniel Prentice. I've been accused of some things in my time, but never of being a stalker! I can assure you that my only intention was to return your keys. You dropped them near my car and didn't hear me calling after you because of that alarm.' He lowered his voice. 'Actually, that chair you're sitting on is Jacobean and rather fragile.'

Cheeks flaming, Louise sprang up and reluctantly took his outstretched hand, looking into dark brown eyes flecked with amber lights that danced with amusement. Now, with a jolt, she noticed his classic good looks and the mass of dark chestnut hair flopping over a rather high forehead. There was a scar on his chin and she wondered how he'd come by it.

'Louise Gresham,' she told him. 'Thanks for returning my keys, but that still doesn't mean you can park your car in the spaces reserved for the museum staff.'

He raised his eyebrows. 'Not even if I *am* staff?'

She stared at him uncertainly and Ryan intervened. 'Nathaniel is going to be standing in for Dr Dakar whilst he's ill. He's come to take a look at our latest Saxon acquisitions,' he informed her.

Light suddenly dawned and there was an embarrassed silence. 'Oh, of course, you're giving the lecture here tonight — in place of Dr Dakar.'

Nathaniel Prentice inclined his head. 'Yes. I've stepped into the breach at the last minute.'

'And I'm sure you'll provide an excellent substitute,' Ryan told him.

'I'll do my best,' Nathaniel assured him, smiling at the young woman standing in front of him. She was slight with silky dark brown hair drawn back rather severely from an oval face. Her long-lashed grey eyes looked sad, and Nathaniel found himself wondering why.

Just then someone beckoned to Ryan and Nathaniel Prentice said: 'Obviously, you're busy at the moment Ryan, so perhaps Miss Gresham will join me for coffee in the cafeteria until you're free.'

Reluctantly, Louise accompanied him into the museum coffee shop. As they sat over cups of cappuccino, she waited for him to enthuse about the Saxon treasures that had recently been unearthed on a nearby building site but, instead, he surprised her by asking, 'So how come you're working here on a temporary basis?'

But, Louise had no intention of

telling him anything about her personal life. 'Oh, I'm covering for someone on maternity leave,' she said briefly.

'Yes, I know — Ryan told me. So what are you planning to do when your job here finishes?'

Louise gave a slight shrug. 'Oh, I expect something will crop up.'

'You'd make an excellent traffic warden,' he told her; eyes twinkling.

'Don't fancy the weather conditions,' she countered. 'Anyway, I'm here for a few months yet.'

'Arranging exhibitions and such-like in the upstairs galleries?'

'Yes, but I also help out as and where I'm needed. Sometimes, when school parties come in, they need an extra pair of hands in the Education Room or even, on occasion, in the gift shop.'

He raised his eyebrows. 'Right — so you must have attended quite a few courses.'

'Just a few.' She sipped her coffee wishing he'd stop asking her so many personal questions. Looking up, she met his gaze steadily and decided to ask a few of her own. 'So, what about you?'

'Me?' It was Nathaniel's turn to look surprised. 'Oh, I'm actually a Keeper of Human History — like Philip Dakar — but I'm also an archaeologist. Philip's an old friend of mine and — as I happen to have a window in my diary on Thursdays — I've agreed to take over his evening lectures on archaeology for the time-being, so that they don't have to be cancelled.'

They sat in silence for a few moments whilst Louise digested this information, and then he told her about a recently excavated Roman site he'd visited the previous week in Yorkshire.

As Ryan reappeared with Stuart Tomlinson, the museum's director, Nathaniel Prentice drained his coffee cup and got to his feet.

'And now, if you'll excuse me I've got a pressing engagement with some Saxon remains. Haven't seen them since the dig!'

He gave her a devastating smile.

'Hopefully, I've proved that I'm harmless.'

Louise stared after him as he walked off in the direction of the Saxon display. He exuded an air of confidence. Not only was he good-looking, but he'd proved to be an interesting companion, and had managed to put her at her ease. She smiled to herself, wondering what Chloe would have to say when she learnt Louise had had coffee with their eminent guest speaker, and of their unfortunate encounter in the car park.

Louise lingered over her coffee for a few minutes longer, deep in thought. She had moved to Whitchurch almost three months ago when her job had disappeared practically overnight. She still couldn't bear to think about it because the circumstances were too painful.

She sighed. Hers had been a classic fairy tale romance to begin with. She'd been working up north in a minor stately home. One day the owner's handsome younger son, Ashley Harper-Jones, had arrived back from his travels abroad and she'd fallen head over heels in love with him.

Ashley's father had indulged his son's whim, financing his latest project — an art gallery in London. Louise had been completely bewitched by Ashley who had whisked her off to London, where she'd always dreamed of working. For the next eighteen months life was bliss, but then harsh reality set in as Ashley began to lose interest in both Louise *and* the gallery.

Things came to a head one day when a glamorous red-head had appeared in the gallery introducing herself as, Erin, and asking for Ashley. Apparently, he'd met her in Australia and run into her again at a recent party.

Within days Ashley announced that he was closing the gallery and leaving Louise for the red-haired Erin. Devastated, Louise had been faced with the choice of returning to her parents who would no doubt have said, '*Told you so,*' or finding herself a new job.

'Are you planning to sit there all day?' enquired a cold voice, cutting across her thoughts.

Startled, Louise looked up to find Arlene Miles, the Exhibitions Officer, and her immediate superior, glowering down at her.

'So sorry, Arlene, I was just about to . . . '

'It may have escaped your notice but it's one fifteen and I've been waiting for you to return from lunch so that I can go off duty. You're being very inconsiderate, Louise.'

Louise got to her feet, deciding not to mention her reason for being a few minutes late. She couldn't understand why Arlene was making such a fuss, because the gallery, where they were currently working, was closed to the public for a few days. Anyway, Louise always stayed until she'd completed her allocated tasks.

Thankfully, just then, another member of staff attracted Arlene's attention and Louise escaped upstairs to the gallery where they were setting up a new exhibition depicting life in and around Whitchurch in the nineteenth century.

As Louise worked, her thoughts turned to Philip Dakar. She had first met him when he had visited the London art gallery. He'd come to see Ashley and she'd heard raised voices and wondered what it was about.

At the time, Louise had been concerned about the argument, but Ashley had assured her it was nothing to worry about — just a difference of opinion between one professional and another.

After that Philip Dakar had visited the gallery on a number of occasions. One day, on his way out, he had thrust his card into her hand and, lowering his voice, had invited her to contact him if ever she considered changing her job. It bore the address of the Whitchurch museum.

Later, when Louise was packing up her belongings, she'd come across the card Dr Dakar had given her and had decided to contact him. Amazingly, he'd told her that there'd be a temporary vacancy when the Assistant Exhibitions Officer went on maternity leave, and that he'd recommend Louise for the post, if she was interested.

Philip had a fair amount of influence and, within a couple of weeks; she'd been called for interview and been offered the job.

Whitchurch was in a pleasant part of Kent. The job at the museum was turning out to be just what she needed for the time-being. It had proved a life-line. No-one asked any questions and, so far as she was aware, Dr Dakar and his wife, Mary, were the only two in Whitchurch with any idea of what had brought her here.

Presently, Louise stood surveying the display area she'd just arranged with a sense of satisfaction. She loved the watercolours by a nineteenth century local artist, and felt pleased with her efforts.

She was just about to call it a day

when Ryan Clarke rushed into the gallery. 'Oh good, you *are* still here!' He smoothed back his fair hair. 'Phew! What a day! I was hoping to come up before this, but I haven't had a moment to breathe!' He glanced around the room. 'Wow! This is looking great, Louise. You've got a real flair.'

'Do you really think so?' she asked, pleased that he'd noticed her efforts.

'Absolutely.' He studied the display; head on one side, blue eyes thoughtful.

'Thanks Ryan — although I can't take all the credit. Arlene is responsible for the area at the front . . . Did you want me for anything in particular?'

'I've decided to go to Nathaniel Prentice's lecture tonight. Stuart Tomlinson's indicated he expects to see the museum staff well-represented so I had no option but to volunteer. How about coming with me?'

Louise, who had been looking forward to a quiet evening in front of the TV, hesitated before replying. She realised she was curious to learn more about Nathaniel Prentice and would be interested to hear his talk.

'Thanks Ryan. I'd like that.

Judging from his broad grin, he was obviously pleased that she'd agreed to accompany him.

* * *

When she'd come to Whitchurch, the Dakars had arranged for Louise to lodge with a friend of theirs. Grace Whitton was a lovely lady who had been widowed a few years back and was glad of the company. Although Grace had no immediate family, she had a large circle of friends. She was prepared to cook supper for Louise and, in exchange, Louise took her shopping. The arrangement suited both of them fine.

Pulling up outside the neat semi-detached house in a tree-lined avenue, Louise hurried indoors. There were tantalising smells coming from the kitchen.

Grace looked up from the cooker, a smile on her pleasant face.

'Ah, there you are, Louise. I'm just about ready to serve up. Hope you don't mind eating early tonight because I'm off to my WI meeting presently.'

'That's fine. I hadn't forgotten.' Louise shrugged off her jacket and began to lay the table. 'Actually, I'm going out as well — back to the museum to a lecture. Dr Dakar was to have taken it but someone called Nathaniel Prentice has stepped in.'

Grace's head shot up again, grey curls bouncing. 'Really? So he *is* able to cover! I knew Mary Dakar had suggested it to Mr Tomlinson, but Nathaniel's such a busy man that she thought it might be too last minute for him to accept.'

'Oh, so you know Mr Prentice, do you?' Louise asked in surprise.

'I certainly do. He's a delightful young man. Have you met him yet?'

'Well, it's funny you should say that, Grace, because . . . ' And Louise told her what had happened at lunch-time.

Grace laughed heartily. 'You're a caution Louise and no mistake.'

Over supper Louise attempted to find out more about Nathaniel Prentice. Grace hesitated. 'Well, he's hardly a stranger to me. He's a friend of the Dakars. As a matter of fact, he used to lodge here way back too — had that room you're in now.'

Louise stared at her in amazement. 'Really! I'd no idea. Tell me more.' But, to her disappointment, Grace wasn't very forthcoming.

'Oh, now that he's based in London I don't see much of him, although he pops up from time to time when there's something of interest to view at the museum.'

There was a curious expression on Grace's face as she added, almost to herself. 'I'm so glad he's offered to help out with Philip Dakar's lectures. After all, it's been a long time and it's not as if anyone there would know . . . '

She trailed off leaving Louise wondering what she'd meant, but some instinct prevented her from asking any more questions just then.

After a quick shower, Louise sorted out a fresh blouse and scrambled back into her navy blue uniform. Peering at her reflection in the mirror, she decided that she'd got an ordinary face; her best features being her long-lashed, large grey eyes and clear, creamy skin. Brushing her silky, dark shoulder-length hair until it shone, she twisted it into a neat top knot.

Ryan turned up promptly at seven o'clock and drove them the short distance to the museum. The lecture room was packed with a cross-section of staff and members of the public. There were seats reserved for their party near the front. Mr Tomlinson was there with his wife and one or two of the other senior members of staff, including Arlene Miles.

The lecture, accompanied by illustrations and photographs, was riveting. Nathaniel Prentice obviously had a keen brain, and his lecture on Roman

Britain was tinged with humour. He told his audience in some detail about the Roman mosaics; with particular emphasis on those in the villa at Lullingstone, which he pointed out were amongst the most well-preserved and important in Britain.

Nathaniel Prentice was an eloquent speaker whose enthusiasm and knowledge was infectious and his audience was captivated.

During the coffee break, Ryan went off to speak with some people he knew and Louise found herself standing beside a young woman.

'He's a brilliant speaker, isn't he?

Louise agreed. 'Yes. He certainly knows his subject and makes it come alive.'

'I'm doing a degree in archaeology,' the young woman informed her. 'It was unfortunate that Dr Dakar was taken ill, but such a treat for us to have Nathaniel Prentice in his place. He's so good looking, isn't he? It's amazing he's still single; although I suspect there

18

must be someone in the background, don't you?'

'I really wouldn't know,' Louise told her shortly, and moving away with a muttered excuse, came face to face with Nathaniel Prentice. She was aware from the amused gleam in his eyes, that he must have been in earshot.

'Hallo, again Louise. Are you enjoying the evening?' he wanted to know.

'Very much, although I have to confess that the idea of grovelling about in a muddy field looking for fragments of pottery and bones, doesn't really appeal to me,' she said honestly.

'I take it you're more interested in displaying the objects aesthetically rather than in discovering them?'

She considered. 'Yes, I think it's just a different perspective. Actually, I *am interested* in archaeology — on a fine day!'

He chuckled and, just then, Ryan joined them. 'Marvellous talk, Nat. You've made me want to go off and take a look at some of those sites you've been telling us about.'

'Good. That was the intention. You need first-hand experience. Anyway, I hope you're going to come up with some leading questions for the second half.'

Ryan's face was a picture and Louise tried not to laugh. She admired Nathaniel's intellect and knew he had given a far more lively talk than Philip Dakar would have done. She had only attended two of Philip's lectures, but that was enough to realise that, whilst he undoubtedly knew his stuff, his delivery was as dry as some of the relics.

Nathaniel kept them on their toes for the rest of the evening with handouts and, at one point, some group discussion. She was impressed and was astonished to find it was ten thirty by the time they wound up.

'That was different,' Ryan commented as he drove her home. 'Old Dakar is going to have his work cut out to match that performance — mind you, Nathaniel was a tad too gimmicky for my liking.'

'I don't agree with you there,' Louise told him. 'He just had a totally different approach from Dr Dakar.'

'Right. I can see you've joined his fan club!'

'Don't be silly! I don't know the man and remember what happened when we first met.'

Ryan laughed. 'Actually, that was quite funny come to think of it. I wonder what our Philip would have to say about that!'

'Hopefully, he won't get to hear about it. He can't be planning to come back any time soon if Nathaniel Prentice has arranged to take over all his lectures for the foreseeable future.

'Yes, that's what I was thinking. You know, I think there's more to this than meets the eye.'

'How d'you mean?' Louise demanded, her stomach churning with apprehension.

'Maybe Philip Dakar's illness is more serious than we thought and he's thinking of taking early retirement.'

Louise's heart plummeted. Philip Dakar had taken her on at the museum and given her back her life. She would always be eternally grateful to him.

'We'll just have to wait and see then, won't we?' she said quietly.

When they pulled up outside Grace's house, Ryan sat chatting for a few minutes, but Louise decided against asking him in.

'I've really enjoyed your company, Louise. Perhaps we can go somewhere that isn't work-related another time.'

Louise knew she'd have to let him down gently and simply said, 'Thanks. It's been an interesting evening.' She was just beginning to settle down in Whitchurch and didn't want the complication of another relationship. Besides, Ryan simply wasn't her type. She was convinced that, apart from work, they'd have absolutely nothing in common.

2

For the next few days, Louise was so busy that she didn't have time to dwell on her own problems. She liked the job in the museum well enough, but disliked being at everyone's beck and call, when previously she'd been used to having more responsibility. It was particularly frustrating when she could see how things might be improved upon.

Her immediate boss, Arlene Miles, was an elegant woman in her late thirties. Arlene tended to be rather unimaginative and stereotyped. She was also extremely pedantic and critical.

Arlene came to stand beside Louise now as she put the finishing touches to a display of sculpture. She pursed her lips. 'Hmm, I'm not convinced that blue is right — rather too vivid — detracts from the items on display.'

'I'm afraid it's all that was available,' Louise told her, trying to keep her cool, but inwardly exasperated. Arlene was always difficult to please.

Turning, Louise almost cannoned into Nathaniel Prentice who was studying the display intently, head on one side.

'Actually, I quite like that backcloth — although, if I might make a suggestion?'

'Of course, Nathaniel, I'd value your expert opinion,' Arlene simpered, flicking back her short blonde hair.

Louise saw the glint in his eyes. He leant forward and removed one of the sculptures. 'In my opinion, this detracts from the others in the display. Now, if you were to find a home for it somewhere else — let's say over there — then that might solve the problem.'

'Well, if that's what you think then I'm happy to take your advice. Sometimes I think one's better off doing the job oneself rather than to delegate; although I have to say Chloe would have understood exactly what was needed.'

Louise felt her cheeks burning and bit back a sharp retort. She'd spent ages on the display. Sometimes Arlene was impossibly difficult to please.

'Actually, Arlene, I've come to ask a favour. I can see you're extremely busy, but I'm wondering if you could possibly spare Louise for half an hour or so — if she's agreeable.'

Louise was startled. She half expected Arlene to refuse, but realised she wouldn't want to lose face in front of such an eminent visitor.

'But of course — if there's an errand she can run for you. She's due a coffee break anyway and, to be honest, I'm going to have to redo some of these displays myself.'

The woman was insufferable and the idea of escaping for a short while was appealing. Louise followed Nathaniel Prentice out of the gallery, wondering what he wanted her to do.

'I'll explain over coffee,' he told her,

seeing her enquiring look. 'Actually, I thought you'd made a perfectly good job of that display.' And he winked at her.

Once they were sitting in a quiet corner of the coffee shop with cappuccinos and almond croissants in front of them, he said, 'If I'm going to be doing these lectures for a few weeks, I'll need someone to help me set them up beforehand. Now, I've had a word with the powers that be and, if you're agreeable, can I borrow you for a couple of hours on Thursday afternoons — what do you say?'

Louise finished her mouthful of pastry. 'Actually, it would have been nice to have been consulted first,' she told him. 'I can't imagine what Arlene Miles will have to say.'

His eyes twinkled. 'Oh, she'll get over it, I imagine? I can tell you've got a real eye for display, Louise.'

'However would you know that?' she asked in surprise.

'I've made it my business to take a

look at the areas you've had a hand in. Besides, Philip Dakar's recommendation is enough for me.'

Louise felt herself colouring. 'Right, I'll naturally do all I can to help.'

'Good. I was hoping you'd say that. I realise this is a bit of an imposition, but I was wondering if you'd be prepared to assist me during the lectures too?'

'I, um . . . ' She only hesitated for moment. 'Yes, I'd be only too pleased to help out.'

Nathaniel spent the next ten minutes filling Louise in with ideas for the following week's lecture. His enthusiasm was catching. She found herself studying him and realised again that he was an incredibly attractive man with that thatch of chestnut hair, finely chiselled features and those animated brown eyes flecked with amber lights. When he smiled he revealed a slight dimple in his chin.

'Can I get you another coffee?'

She pulled herself together with difficulty. 'Oh, no thank you. I'd best be getting back. Shall I leave it to you to speak to Arlene Miles?'

'Yes I'll sort it out with Arlene. I can't see any problem. Until Thursday then.'

As Louise had anticipated and, contrary to what Nathaniel had thought, Arlene Miles was not best pleased.

'I've told Mr Prentice that you might be needed to set up an exhibition in another part of the museum. I *am* supposed to be the coordinator, but no-one would ever think it.'

Arlene sniffed her disapproval and spent the rest of the morning finding fault with everything Louise did. She was relieved when the afternoon came round and she was sent to help out in the natural history gallery where a group of school children were on an educational visit.

That evening Louise had a phone call from Chloe asking if she'd like to call round the following day which she happened to have off.

* * *

The next morning was wet and windy and not the sort of weather to take a tiny baby out. Chloe was pleased to see her.

'Hi — come in. I'm really looking forward to a good girly natter. You can fill me in with all that's been going on at the museum. Much as I love Ava, one sided baby conversation is not exactly the most stimulating in the world!'

Ava was a pretty baby with a quantity of dark hair. Louise nursed her whilst Chloe went to make the coffee, and was captivated by the tiny fingers that curled round hers. Ava snuggled up against her, making tiny baby noises and Louise felt a sudden surge of maternal warmth within her.

Ashley had made it clear, early on in their relationship, that he wasn't keen on children. Louise, finding this hard to believe, had been convinced that, with a little gentle persuasion on her part, he would change his mind. With hindsight, she realised that he was too much of a party animal to take on the responsibility of being a father and, although quite a bit older than her, was still immature in some ways.

Louise handed Ava over reluctantly to Chloe so that she could put her back in her cot.

'She'll probably settle down for a bit until her next feed. Everyone tells me how fortunate I am to have such a contented baby, but it's still very early days . . . Now come on — fill me in with all the latest hot gossip!'

Louise regaled her new friend with one or two anecdotes; filled her in with what had been happening regarding the latest exhibition and, lastly, brought her up to speed with Nathaniel Prentice taking over Dr Dakar's lectures whilst he was ill.

Chloe's eyebrows shot up. 'Nathaniel Prentice? Wow! There's a blast from the past!'

'How d'you mean?' There was

something in Chloe's tone of voice that intrigued Louise.

Chloe tossed back her mane of sandy hair and passed the biscuits. 'Oh, nothing. It was all before my time and that of most of the management staff — such as Ryan and Arlene and even Stuart.'

'You've wetted my curiosity now! Come on Chloe, if I'm going to do some work for the man you'd better tell me what you're hinting at!'

Chloe hesitated. 'Oh, it's nothing that need concern you, but just a friendly word of warning — Arlene Miles went on a course Nathaniel Prentice was running a while back, and came back singing his praises. She told us they'd shared a table at meal-times and had a lot in common.'

Louise gave her a wry smile. 'OK, thanks for that, but I'm hardly likely to run after him. Anyway, we got off to a bad start. I almost forgot to tell you . . . ' Chloe rocked with laughter, only stopping when little baby Ava began to protest.

'Whoops! Sorry honey! Your mummy's being a bit noisy, isn't she?'

The child soon settled and Louise wondered what on earth Chloe had been about to tell her. 'Come on. You can't leave it there. Tell me what it is you know about Nathaniel Prentice.'

There was a pause. 'Oh, it's just that he's got a bit of history,' she said at last. 'I suppose I might as well tell you before someone else does. Years back, when he was newly qualified, he worked at the museum. I only know because I'm a local girl and my parents told me. Apparently he . . . '

A loud peal on the doorbell left her trailing off in mid-sentence. 'That'll be one of the mums — mine or Tim's — would you be an angel and let her in.'

It turned out to be Chloe's mother, Julie, standing on the step laden with carrier bags. After a few minutes chatting over more coffee, Louise got to her feet and made her excuses, feeling that mother and daughter needed some quality time together with little Ava.

Louise could have wished Julie's timing had been a bit different, as she was dying to know what revelation Chloe had been about to make regarding Nathaniel Prentice. She hadn't liked to broach the subject amidst all the baby talk, and decided it would have to wait until her next visit.

On Sunday morning, Louise accompanied Grace to church and then they had lunch together. In the afternoon Grace was visiting a friend and after dropping her off, Louise decided to drive to a nearby garden centre to purchase a few alpines as a surprise for her friend.

Although very active for her age, Grace had confessed to Louise that she was finding gardening difficult due to arthritis. Louise enjoyed gardening and was happy to lend a hand.

After browsing happily for a time, she selected half a dozen of the delicate little plants and decided to have a cup of tea before returning home. To her amazement, she saw Nathaniel Prentice sitting at a table in the cafeteria with a smartly dressed lady with beautifully coiffured platinum — blonde hair. He waved and came across.

'Hallo there. You're welcome to join us. My mother would like to meet you.'

Louise couldn't very well refuse. She'd already realised that Nathaniel could be gently persuasive, and was obviously used to getting his own way. He picked up her tray and she had no choice but to follow him over to his table where he made the introductions.

Celeste Prentice smiled, putting her at her ease. 'So you're Philip's protégée. He's been singing your praises. Do sit down and tell me about yourself.'

Louise's heart sank as she sensed she was about to be interrogated. The Dakars had been very kind to her, but not intrusive. They were, of course, aware of the way she'd been treated by Ashley, but apart from one or two sympathetic comments, had made very little reference to it.

'I've been staying with my daughter, Serena, in Surrey. Nathaniel collected me from the station and we had an early lunch before coming here.'

Louise smiled and murmured something appropriate before sipping her tea. She found it rather endearing to think that Nathaniel was prepared to spend his precious free time driving his mother to a garden centre. She wondered if they lived together. Surely not! Although pleasant enough, Mrs Prentice seemed rather bossy.

'So what brought you to Whitchurch, Louise?' she asked now.

The cake suddenly tasted like sawdust in Louise's mouth. 'Oh, I just fancied a change of scenery. I'm a country girl at heart, and being in London wasn't really what I'd expected.'

Mrs Prentice picked up her cup. Louise noticed that her eyes were brown like her sons but didn't have the amber flecks.

'So have you any family? I can tell from your accent you're not a Londoner.'

Nathaniel laughed. 'My mother has an insatiable curiosity about people, so don't tell her anything you'd rather not.'

Celeste smiled good-naturedly. 'My son is the biggest tease . . . isn't that apple cake to die for!'

Louise nodded and finishing her mouthful set down her pastry fork. 'Absolutely wonderful. To answer your question, I come from Yorkshire, which I'm sure is very obvious really. I've got one married sister.'

'So, how come you know the Dakars?'

Louise crumbled the remainder of her cake. 'I used to work in an art gallery when I was living in London. Dr Dakar visited occasionally. He gave me his card and told me to get in touch if ever I fancied a change. The gallery closed — so here I am.'

She was aware that Nathaniel was listening intently. He was leaning back on his chair, a thoughtful expression on his face.

'The Dakars have been very kind to me,' Louise added. 'It's a pity Dr Dakar's ill.'

'Yes, indeed, but very fortunate that Nathaniel was available to take his place for this series of lectures,' Celeste commented.

'Oh, I'm sure they'd have found someone else to step in,' Nathaniel said lightly.

'The Dakars seem to be dogged by misfortune,' Celeste commented and Louise intercepted the look Nathaniel shot his mother, and wondered what it was all about. He adeptly changed the subject to gardening.

Nathaniel was amazingly knowledgeable about plants and told Louise about an alpine garden he had visited in the area. Presently, Mrs Prentice announced that she was going to freshen up.

'You mustn't mind if my mother's a bit inquisitive,' Nathaniel told Louise when his parent was out of earshot. 'She used to be a researcher for an MP, so it's second nature to her.'

Louise gave a little smile wondering what the Dakars had told him about her. She was sure she could rely on their discretion, but they would obviously have needed to have said something.

She would ask Chloe what she'd meant about Nathaniel having some history. Did it concern a wife or a partner perhaps? But the young woman who had spoken to her at his lecture on Thursday had said he was single. Anyway, why ever should it matter to her? She'd had enough of men to last her a lifetime!

'I went to see Chloe and the baby yesterday,' she told him — intent on directing the conversation away from herself.

He wrinkled his brow. 'Chloe? Oh, of course, you mean Chloe Sanders — the girl you're covering for. Did you two know each other before you came to Whitchurch?'

Louise shook her head. 'I didn't know anyone here at all — except for

Dr Dakar, but everyone's been very friendly.'

Apart from Arlene Miles, she added silently to herself. She had absolutely no idea why the older woman had taken against her, and assumed it must be a clash of personalities. Arlene had obviously got on well enough with Chloe.

Celeste returned to the table just then and looking at her, Louise admired her beautiful make-up and expertly styled hair. She seemed too young to have a son of Nathaniel's age. According to Chloe he had to be about thirty five — six years older than Louise.

'So nice to meet you, Louise. I'll look forward to seeing you again, my dear,' Celeste told her.

'Yes, Louise is likely to be around for a few months yet,' Nathaniel informed her. 'See you next Thursday, Louise, if not before.'

Louise watched as they left the cafeteria. Nathaniel towered above his mother. The week stretched ahead and it seemed a long time until Thursday afternoon. Louise suddenly wished she was going with them and felt very alone.

* * *

'Celeste Prentice,' I haven't seen her in ages,' Grace told her over supper that evening. 'Such a nice woman — and you say Nathaniel was with her, Louise?'

She nodded. 'Apparently, Mrs Prentice had just been to visit her daughter.

'Serena married well. It's a pity Nathaniel — but then . . . '

Louise looked at her questioningly, but Grace obviously thought better of what she'd been about to say and changed the subject.

'Mary Dakar popped in for a short while this afternoon. A friend of Philip's was visiting him in hospital so she was able to have a bit of a breather. Apparently, Philip's doing very well, but it's likely to be a long haul. It wouldn't surprise me if he took early retirement. Mary Dakar looked very drawn but the break did her good . . . Now, if you've had enough salad; I've got a trifle in the fridge and there's some of that fruit cake in the tin if you care to fetch it.'

As Louise collected up the dirty plates, she wondering what it was people found it so difficult to say about Nathaniel Prentice. She resolved to ask Chloe at the first opportunity.

3

The following morning was chaotic. 'You look fed up,' Ryan told her, as she made to dash past him on the way to the gallery with an armful of worksheets.

She paused. 'No — just rushed off my feet! I don't know where everyone's coming from today. I haven't even had a coffee break.'

'I think Arlene's taking advantage of you, Louise. She was down in the cafeteria earlier chatting to her friends. You're too good natured — that's your trouble.'

'Oh, I don't mind really. After all, it's better to be busy than quiet and I might as well earn my keep.'

Ryan laughed. 'You certainly do that all right. Tell you what. Arlene can't expect you to work through lunch as well. There's a nice coffee shop just round the corner from here and we could escape for a short while.'

Louise couldn't think of any good reason to refuse, especially when Arlene greeted her with a sour look and said, 'I thought you'd got lost in the cafeteria.'

'Actually, I haven't even had a break this morning,' Louise told her quietly, setting down the pile of papers on the corner of a table and beginning to sort them. 'There was a queue for the photocopier.'

'Right — then, in future, don't let the hand-outs get so low. Oh, I suppose you might as well go for an early lunch. You're needed in the education room this afternoon to help with that party of school children.'

Ryan was in a position to arrange his own lunch times and, presently, as they sat in the colourful courtyard garden of a nearby coffee shop, they could have been a million miles away from the hustle and bustle of the small town.

'I've got a couple of tickets for the local Am Dram,' he told her presently in between bites of his sandwich. 'My sister's taking part. It's a comedy — *The Vicar of Dibley*. Remember the television series? I can promise it'll be hilarious. Would you like to come with me?'

Louise found herself saying, yes . . . but then he dropped the bombshell.

'It's on Thursday night — starts at eight o'clock . . . ' He trailed off as he saw her expression. 'What's wrong?'

'Oh, Ryan, I'm sorry, but I've got a prior engagement. I've already arranged to assist Nathaniel Prentice on Thursday evening.'

Ryan scowled. 'Surely he can find someone else to help with his lecture. Tell him you've got a better offer.'

But Louise shook her head. 'Sorry, but a promise is a promise.'

Ryan set his drink down with a splash. 'I suppose I might be able to swap the tickets, although it's a bit late in the day, and they're selling out like hotcakes. Right, I'll get back to you.'

From then on Ryan seemed rather quiet. She wasn't sorry to have upset him, and she could have rearranged but chose not to.

*   *   *

The following day Louise discovered that Arlene was on a course in London. She'd neglected to mention it to Louise, but had left copious notes of what needed doing.

'Typical!' Louise muttered crossly to herself, as she began to tackle the first task; but then she soon became engrossed in her work which she found satisfying.

*   *   *

When Louise turned up to help Nathaniel on Thursday afternoon; she found him busily delving into cardboard boxes. He straightened up. 'Hallo Louise. Now, before we get involved with this, I understand Ryan asked you out to the theatre tonight.'

She felt embarrassed. Why on earth had Ryan mentioned it? 'Yes, but I've told him I'm working here this evening.'

Nathaniel smiled at her. 'But you're not! I've had a word with Arlene and she's happy to step in for this week. She was coming to my lecture anyway, so just you go off and enjoy yourself!'

Louise was speechless. How could Ryan have been so high-handed as to have reorganised her evening like that, without even consulting her? It was shades of Ashley all over again, and she wasn't going to stand for it.

'What's wrong?' Nathaniel asked. 'You don't look very pleased.'

'That's because I'm not used to people sorting things out without consulting me,' she burst out indignantly. 'I'd already arranged to be here this evening and I stick to my word.'

Nathaniel nodded. 'Ryan told me that's what you'd say. Anyway, it's no problem. It's all sorted, so you go off and enjoy your evening — unless . . . '

He gave her a searching glance before asking, 'Louise, do you need the overtime?'

Louise drew herself up to her full height, eyes sparkling with indignation. 'No, I most certainly do not. Not that it's any of your business!'

'True,' he conceded, surprised by her reaction. 'I thought I was doing you a good turn, but I've obviously got it wrong. Apologies. I always seem to be treading on your toes.'

Inwardly seething, Louise was determined not to let her feelings affect her work, and carried out the tasks as efficiently as she could, completing the displays in record time.

'That looks extremely professional, Louise, you certainly know your stuff! Shall we go for a well-earned cup of tea before the cafeteria closes?'

He was standing so close to her that she was extremely aware of him, and felt her pulse quickening. This man was seriously attractive. Louise took a step to one side, pretending to examine a poster.

Louise felt inexplicably disappointed that she wasn't going to be there to assist Nathaniel that evening, but realised Arlene was probably far more accustomed to helping out at lectures, than herself. She knew it was hardly Nathaniel's fault if he had misconstrued the situation.

Presently, they were sitting over tea and biscuits in the cafeteria when Arlene came in. She raised her eyebrows slightly.

'So this is where you are! I came to take over so that you could leave early, Louise, in order to get yourself prettied up for your date with Ryan.'

'We've finished. Louise is worth her weight in gold, Arlene, but thanks anyway,' Nathaniel said airily. 'Can I get you a cup of tea?'

Arlene seemed put out. 'No, thank you. There's plenty I can find to do if you don't need my services. What time shall I get back here this evening?'

'Shall we say sevenish? Thanks Arlene.' He treated her to one of his charming smiles.

Just then Ryan came into the cafeteria and, spotting them, came across.

'She's all yours, Ryan,' Arlene told him sweetly. 'Enjoy your evening.'

Louise could have done with another cup of tea but, with muttered thanks, got to her feet and followed Ryan out into the museum.

'Don't you ever put me in that situation again,' she exploded.

Ryan looked surprised. 'I'm not sure what I'm supposed to have done, Louise.'

You've revamped my arrangements for this evening, that's what! I've never been so embarrassed in my life,' she told him crossly.

Ryan put up his hands in protest. 'Whoa, just hold it there. I was on that course with Arlene on Tuesday and, when she heard you couldn't go to the theatre tonight, she jumped at the chance to take your place. She and Nathaniel get on pretty well — in case you haven't noticed.'

'Then it's a pity he didn't ask her to help out in the first place, isn't it?' she said tartly. 'You do realise I had to learn about all this from Mr Prentice.'

'Sorry, I did try to contact you, but I don't have your mobile number.'

Ryan looked contrite and Louise realised that Arlene had probably manipulated the situation to her advantage. Given the choice, Louise knew she'd have preferred to have been in his company, rather than Ryan's that evening. She simmered down, realising she was being ungracious.

'OK, but in future I'll sort things out for myself, thank you very much!' Ryan looked relieved. 'Got the message! What time shall I pick you up?'

'Oh, no need. I've already arranged to give Grace a lift to the theatre.'

He looked at her in disbelief. 'You mean to say Grace is going to be at the theatre this evening?'

'Yes, she's meeting up with a friend of hers.'

'Right. So you'll be well-chaperoned then!'

'What? Oh don't be silly, Ryan. I doubt if we'll be sitting anywhere near her.' For a moment, she considered making some excuse not to go — saying she had a bad headache, but decided that an evening out would do her good.

'Tell you what, Ryan. Let's meet for a drink in the bar before the show starts — and thanks for asking me.'

Presently, as she showered, Louise reflected that she'd probably been a bit unjust to blame Ryan for rearranging her evening. It was apparent that Arlene had jumped in so that she could assist Nathaniel with his lecture. Louse told herself she was being silly to mind so much. After all, why would Nathaniel care whether Louise helped him or not? He'd probably prefer Arlene anyway.

As she blow-dried her hair, Louise wondered if she was beginning to get over Ashley or whether it was just that Nathaniel Prentice exuded the sort of charm that was enough to make any woman go weak at the knees. No, she'd be much better settling for a night out with Ryan.

Louise enjoyed the theatre far more than she would have believed possible.

It was an extremely good amateur production and very funny. Afterwards, whilst Grace and her friend, Anne, went for another coffee, Ryan took Louise backstage to meet his sister and the rest of the cast.

Holly was a bubbly extrovert who obviously got on well with her brother. She wasted no time in introducing Louise to the rest of the cast; most of whom it seemed Ryan knew already.

'We're having a bit of a party at my place on Sunday — birthday bash. I'll be twenty five! You're welcome to come along if you're free, Louise. It's an open invitation so just turn up. Ryan will give you the address.'

As Holly turned away to greet some more friends Louise touched his arm, 'It's been great meeting everyone, Ryan, but I'll have to go now. The bar closes shortly, and I don't want to leave Grace hanging about. I've thoroughly enjoyed the evening — thanks so much.' And she realised that she genuinely meant it.

As they retraced their steps along the now deserted corridor, Ryan suddenly caught hold of Louise in a tight embrace and kissed her.

'I've been longing to do that for weeks,' he told her. 'You're looking absolutely gorgeous tonight.'

A flood of emotions filled Louise. It was such a short time since she'd been in a relationship with Ashley. Too soon to get involved with anyone else and, although she liked Ryan well enough as a friend, and for the occasional date, she already realised she'd never be that interested in him romantically. Besides, what was the point in getting too involved when her future in Whitchurch was so uncertain?

'Ahem!'

They sprang apart like a couple of guilty teenagers to find a security guard grinning at them. He went off whistling to himself. The colour flooded Louise's cheeks. Ryan laughed.

'I'd like to get to know you better, Louise. I enjoy being with you and think we could have a good time together.'

She forced a smile but deliberately kept her distance. 'But I'm not a good-time girl,' she quipped. 'Besides, we're work colleagues.'

'Why on earth should that matter? What about Nathaniel Prentice and Arlene Miles? It's obvious she's got a crush on him and he's not exactly discouraging her, otherwise she would hardly have volunteered to have taken your place tonight, would she?'

Louise swallowed. 'Right — well, I've enjoyed tonight, Ryan but . . . '

He touched her arm. 'It's okay, I get the message — you'd prefer to take things more slowly. I find you attractive, Louise. You must have realised that.'

She opened her mouth to say something, but just then they rounded a corner and, to her relief, she saw an anxious-looking Grace standing in the vestibule.

'Oh, thank goodness! I was beginning to wonder where you were. I insisted

Anne didn't hang about.'

They walked the short distance to the car-park, discussing the play. Ryan stood waving as they drove off. Louise had to admit she'd found him good company, and he'd certainly got a knack of making her feel special. He'd helped her to restore confidence in herself and that had to be a good thing.

Louise found herself lying awake as a medley of thoughts buzzed about her head. She knew it was going to take time to get over Ashley, but hadn't expected to feel quite so unresponsive when Ryan kissed her. She knew she had to move on, but perhaps she wasn't ready — not quite yet.

Just as she'd decided this, she had an image of Nathaniel Prentice, tall good-looking with those expressive dark eyes — and a voice like honey. He was more mature than either Ashley or Ryan and, in the short space of time that she'd known him, she'd found him entering her thoughts more and more.

On Saturday afternoon, Grace asked Louise if she'd take her to the hospital to see Philip Dakar. He was apparently feeling much better now and requesting company.

When they arrived, Philip Dakar, although frail, was looking considerably better than Louise had expected. He was fully dressed and sitting in a chair in a side ward. He smiled as they entered, and stretched out his hands to them His wife was busily arranging his get-well cards.

'So kind of people, but we're running out of space.' She said.

Philip wanted to know all about the museum, but they were anxious not to overtire him. 'So how's Nathaniel Prentice coping with my lectures?'

'Philip, Nat came in yesterday evening and told you all about it!' Mary protested.

'Yes, but that was his version. I want to know from a member of the audience.'

'I'm afraid I was only present at last week's lecture,' Louise told him, and explained what had happened.

'Ah, so young Ryan's taken you out on a date, has he?'

'It was hardly a date,' Grace chipped in. 'Ryan's sister is taking a major part in the local amateur dramatics and handed out some complimentary tickets.'

'It was a very enjoyable evening but, unfortunately, it clashed with the lecture. Anyway, I'll definitely be there next Thursday,' Louise assured him.

'So Arlene helped out. Well! Well!' Mary Dakar raised her eyebrows.

Just then the door opened and Nathaniel Prentice came into the room.

'Goodness your ears must be burning,' Mary told him. 'Louise was just telling us how well you've been coping with the lectures.'

'What you really mean *is* — Philip has been quizzing her about my shortcomings!'

'I was wondering when we'd run into

one another,' she said.

'Sorry, Grace, I've been neglecting you.'

'Oh, I know how busy you are . . . So have you still got your flat in London?'

'Yes, but I've also found myself a country residence in this neck of the woods.'

'Tell me more,' Grace urged.

'Do you remember my friend, Matt Evans?'

Grace chuckled. 'How could I forget? Nat and Matt. What a duo! I could tell you some stories from those days, Louise.'

'Please don't, Nathaniel pleaded, or I'll lose the best assistant I've ever had.'

Grace laughed and Philip and Mary Dakar joined in.

'Oh, we've grown up since then! Matt's off on his travels again for a few months, and he's given me the use of his cottage when I'm in this area. It's a bit out in the sticks, but suits me fine and, in exchange, I'll be keeping an eye on the place, dealing with his mail etc.'

'Sounds like a good arrangement to me,' Mary Dakar told him. 'We weren't expecting to see you today, Nat.'

Nathaniel was aware that Louise was taking in every word. He had a sudden inspiration. There was a problem regarding the following day and he wondered if she'd be prepared to help. He'd enjoy getting to know her better. Philip Dakar had a reputation for helping people with problems. He'd been very reticent when Nathaniel had mentioned Louise, just saying that the gallery she'd been working in up in London had closed down and she'd needed a change. Nathaniel suspected there was rather more to the story than Philip was prepared to tell him.

'I'm afraid there's a bit of a problem regarding tomorrow, Mary. My mother's got some friends over from America. It seems this weekend is the only time they can all meet up. She didn't know until yesterday. I could go on my own and would be more than happy to do so, but seeing Louise has given me an idea and I was wondering . . . '

Grace had given a signal that it was time to leave, and Louise paused in the act of fastening her jacket as she wondered what he was about to say.

Philip Dakar looked across at Louise, a worried expression on his face. 'I wonder, my dear, if you happened to be free tomorrow, whether you could do us a very great favour?'

'Yes, of course I will. 'Mystified, Louise looked from one to the other.

'You can turn it down if you like, dear. It's a bit of an imposition,' Mary told her.

Louise, who was nearly bursting with curiosity, wished they would just come out with it and looked imploringly at Nathaniel.

'Don't worry, it's nothing too demanding,' he assured her.

Philip nodded towards his wife. 'Well, it's rather a big favour. You see our granddaughter is away at boarding school and tomorrow is her thirteenth birthday. We had planned to take her out to celebrate her becoming a teenager, but I've put the kibosh on that, I'm afraid. Nathaniel's offered to take Marilena and her young friend out for the day, and his mother was going to accompany him.'

Louise's pulse was racing unaccountably. She realised it was a spur of the moment invitation from Nathaniel, asking her to take Celeste's place, and was tempted to suggest that perhaps he'd rather ask Arlene Miles instead.

Grace gave Louise an encouraging smile and she felt she could hardly refuse. The Dakars had been so good to her since she'd arrived in Whitchurch. She'd like to do something for them for a change.

'I'd be only too pleased to help out,' she told them with a smile. There were dozens of questions she wanted to ask, but she realised they'd have to wait. The Dakars looked so relieved.

Nathaniel arranged to pick Louise up from Grace's house in the morning. Philip Dakar suddenly looked very tired and they took this as a signal to leave.

'Well, you can certainly look forward to a different sort of day, Louise,' Grace said as soon as they were out of earshot.

'Mmm, I'm not quite sure how that happened,' Louise mused. 'Not that I mind helping the Dakars out. They've been so kind to me. So tell me, Grace, where are their granddaughter's parents?'

There was a curious expression on Grace's face. For a moment or two she didn't reply and then she said, 'Fleur, the Dakar's daughter and Marilena's mother died soon after the child was born, and there's a bit of a question mark as to who the father is. I don't want to betray a confidence so we'd better leave it at that for now.

'No doubt the Dakars will fill you in when they feel the time is right. So far as Marilena's concerned she has no living parents. The Dakars are all she's ever known but because they're so much older, they thought it would do the girl good to mix with others of her own age — hence the boarding school.'

'Right, but how come Nathaniel Prentice is involved?' Louise asked, puzzled.

'Marilena is very fond of Nathaniel — thinks of him as an uncle whom she also doesn't have — at least, not one who acknowledges her. Besides, Nat's her godfather.'

'Really? Oh, that explains it then.'

'No, you'll find it doesn't actually explain anything,' Grace said mysteriously. 'Now, I don't know about you, but I'm gasping for a cup of tea. It was so hot in that hospital. Can we stop off on the way home?'

4

It wasn't until they were sitting over tea and cake in a rather nice tea shop situated just outside of Whitchurch then Grace suddenly said, 'Didn't you tell me you'd been invited to Ryan's sister's party tomorrow evening?'

Louise clapped her hand to her mouth. 'Oh, I'd clean forgotten! I seem to have double booked myself with the same two people all over again!'

'Well, if you've forgotten then you can't have been that keen to have gone in the first place,' Grace observed drily.

'Actually, you're quite right,' Louise admitted. 'Anyway, I haven't definitely accepted. Ryan said he'd be in touch when he got back from his cricket match tomorrow. Perhaps I'll be able to do both, but it'll rather depend on what time I get home.'

'Well, Marilena's school isn't exactly

round the corner; it's in Sussex,' Grace informed her.

'Right,' Louise said. 'So, why would Nathaniel ask me along? Won't the girls find it a bit strange?'

Grace laughed. 'Why ever would they? Nathaniel's entitled to have a friend. Anyway, I'm sure Mary is relieved to know you're going to be there. Marilena might prefer to have a woman to talk to if she's got any problems.'

Louise had to be content with that. After they had finished their tea they found a gift shop nearby and Louise purchased some ethnic beads which Grace assured her Marilena would like. She also bought some funky earrings for Holly, just in case she managed to get to her party.

*　*　*

Louise was undecided what to wear for the following day's excursion and finally settled on dark blue trousers, a white tunic top and a lightweight pink jacket. She tied her gleaming dark hair back in a ponytail and stepped into a pair of black sandals.

Nathaniel was punctual. He looked as smart as ever, dressed in a pale green jacket and grey trousers with an open-necked striped green shirt and green tie.

It was a beautiful day in early summer and the drive through the Kent countryside and into Sussex was pleasant.

'Now, I don't know how much you've been told about Marilena,' Nathaniel said presently.

'Very little. I understand that she's been brought up by her grandparents and that she hasn't any other family.'

Nathaniel nodded. 'Not any that acknowledges her. She's going through a bit of a difficult patch at the moment, which is why the Dakars were a bit dubious when I offered to step in. They never want to put upon people. Marilena is a lovely girl, but she can be a bit wilful and her marks haven't been very good just recently.'

'Is there any particular reason?' Louise asked, wondering what she'd let herself in for.

'Not that we're aware of. Sometimes it's easier to talk to strangers, isn't it? And you seem a fairly sympathetic person. Anyway, let's play it all by ear, shall we?'

By the time they arrived at the school housed in an old stately home, Louise was feeling more than a little apprehensive. They were ushered into the library by one of the staff, and a tray of coffee was brought to them whilst Marilena was summonsed.

Marilena Dakar was slight and extremely pretty with a heart-shaped face, huge brown eyes and thick honey-coloured hair. Louise was aware that, by the time the girl was much older, she would be a beauty.

Beyond a cool greeting, Marilena's entire attention was taken up with Nathaniel, and by opening the presents he had brought for her. Louise occupied herself by studying the paintings adorning the walls of the library.

Nathaniel asked, 'So where shall we go then? Any ideas? And what's happened to your friend Sophy?'

Marilena was prevented from replying when the door opened and the head-teacher, Miss Hardy; an elegant grey-haired lady came into the room. After shaking their hands and exchanging greetings she asked Nathaniel if she might have a word with him in private.

Left alone with Louise, Marilena sat studying her shoes whilst the minutes ticked by. At last Louise said, 'Come on Marilena, tell me what the problem is — has it got something to do with your friend, Sophy? Have you fallen out with her?'

Marilena's head shot up in surprise. 'How did you guess?'

'Probably because I was your age once. Don't you want her to come out with us today?'

'It's not like that — you wouldn't understand,' the girl muttered sullenly.

'Come on, tell me,' Louise coaxed gently. 'You might be pleasantly surprised.'

Marilena hesitated and then said in a rush. 'I'm hopeless at Maths and Sophy's not much better. Yesterday we had to re-do our work because we got such low marks. We knew the answers were in our teacher's desk drawer so we copied them. Sophy got caught putting them back, and I let her take all the blame. She's got to stay behind as a punishment and is in a mega strop with me. I felt bad about it so I've owned up now.'

Louise tried to look stern, inwardly relieved that it wasn't anything more serious. 'Right, well that wasn't clever of you, was it? I don't condone cheating, but if you don't understand what you've got to do then you probably both need some extra tuition.'

Marilena sniffed. 'You don't know our Maths teacher. He only has time for the top sets. If we ask him to explain again he says we weren't concentrating.

He's a rubbish teacher anyway.'

Privately, Louise thought there had to be some truth in that. 'I'm sure Nathaniel will sort things out.'

'I thought I was going to have a brilliant birthday, but things aren't turning out how I expected. I'm worried about my grandfather. Supposing he dies . . . '

Louise looked at the forlorn young face, and her heart went out to her. 'He's not going to die for many years yet. I went to see him yesterday and so did your Uncle Nathaniel. I can assure you, your grandfather will be as good as new after a rest.'

There was another silence and then Marilena said, 'Uncle Nat has never brought one of his girlfriends here before, so he must be serious about you.'

Louise coloured. 'Oh, no, I'm not his girlfriend. We're just work colleagues and, as I know your grandparents, he invited me along.'

Marilena tried to process this. 'Right.

I suppose Uncle Nat thought Sophy and I might be too much of a handful for him on his own. Last time he visited, a couple of sixth-formers asked if he was my father. I had to tell them, unfortunately *no*, but I really wish he was. I don't know anything about my father — even less than my mother. Weird, isn't it? If I could choose, I'd choose Uncle Nat.'

Louise smiled and decided it was time to change the subject.

'Oh, I nearly forgot. I've brought you a little birthday present. I wanted to wait until you'd opened all your family presents.'

Marilena seemed to really like the necklace and put it on straight away. 'Wow! My mother would have been really made up with this! Grandma said she loved Africa and spent a few months there before going to Uni. When I'm older I'm going to follow in her footsteps and do a gap year there — so that I can see it all for myself.'

Louise wondered if she would say

any more about her mother but the girl was fingering the beads and seemed to have a faraway look in her eyes. A few minutes later Nathaniel returned looking serious.'

'Why didn't you tell us you were finding your Maths difficult, Marilena?' he asked. 'Your head teacher is going to move you into a different set on my recommendation.'

'What about Sophy? I'm not going without Sophy!' Marilena looked belligerent.

'Miss Hardy is going to speak to Sophy's aunt about moving her, too. Now, I've managed to do a bit of bargaining with Miss Hardy. As it's your birthday she's going to allow the pair of you to come out with us today, but, in exchange, you must both attend an extra Maths class tomorrow.'

Impetuously, Marilena threw her arms round Nathaniel's neck. 'You're the best uncle anyone could possibly have.'

He laughed. 'Right — now you'd

better have a word with Miss Hardy — and then go and find Sophy and say sorry for dropping her in it, and then we'll go before there's any more delay.'

'The problem is — these academic types are brilliant in their own field, but often can't get their subject across,' Nathaniel commented when Marilena had gone in search of her friend. 'It seems Miss Hardy is well aware of the situation — not that it excuses what the girls did.'

When Marilena arrived with Sophy; a rather plump blonde-haired girl, Nathaniel said briskly, 'OK — let's put this unfortunate episode behind us and start again, shall we? Where do you two girls want to go?'

'Brighton!' they chorused in unison.

Nathaniel widened his eyes. 'Really? I'd have thought you'd have had enough of looking round the Pavilion, but obviously not.'

Marilena pulled a face. 'Not the Pavilion! We've been there at least three times with my grandparents. It's one of

Grandpa's favourite places *and* we've been to all the museums more than once.'

'And the Sea Life Centre — although that was fun,' Sophy chipped in.

'Right, so what *had* you got in mind?'

The two girls exchanged glances and Marilena said, 'After lunch, we thought perhaps — the pier?'

'I suppose you're after the amusement arcade and the funfair?'

They nodded and Nathaniel winked at Louise and said in an undertone, 'Rather tackier than the Dakars would normally allow.'

'And then perhaps we could go bowling — and we know it's Sunday, but lots of the shops will probably be open and so we were wondering . . . '

Nathaniel spread his hands in a gesture of mock horror. 'Aw, not the dreaded shops! You know, I bet Louise hasn't been to the Pavilion, have you?'

'No, and they tell me it's an absolute must if you're in this area,' Louise replied, seeing Nathaniel's expression and playing along with him.

The two girls looked downcast until they realised the adults were winding them up and then they laughed.

'However do you suppose we'll fit all that in?' Nathaniel asked. 'Come on let's have lunch first and then we'll decide. I don't know about you, but I could eat a horse, and I've had strict instructions to take you for a cream tea before we come back here! Your grandfather's treating you both, Marilena.'

Their eyes lit up. 'Yay — just the pier and shops then! Perhaps we can go bowling another time,' Marilena said.

'I'll bring you again, Louise, and take you to see the *Pavilion* and the *Lanes* where all the antique shops are — when we have a bit of peace and quiet away from noisy school girls.'

'Uncle Nat!' They saw his expression and burst out laughing.

After the unfortunate beginning, the girls had an enjoyable day. Marilena was still wearing the necklace and Louise could see that now the girl was more relaxed; she was a lively character with a sense of fun. Sophy was a polite, amiable sort of girl who obviously followed Marilena's lead.

Louise and Nathaniel kept the girls in sight but tried not to cramp their style. This proved tiring as the two youngsters zipped up and down escalators in the shops, paraded in front of mirrors holding expensive clothes in front of them, and spent at least ten minutes trying on outrageous fascinator headgear. As a stony-faced assistant began to move in their direction, Louise rapidly removed the girls from the department.

'Enough!' Nathaniel told them, trying to keep a straight face. 'Let's go to the pier before they throw us out of here!'

It proved to be one of the most hilarious days Louise could remember for a long time. She couldn't help wondering what on earth Arlene Miles would think if she were to see them now. Louise couldn't imagine that lady unbending sufficiently to go in an amusement arcade with a couple of teenagers.

Later over tea and cream cakes, the girls started discussing the summer holidays. 'Sophy's parents are taking her on a trip to Italy,' Marilena announced.

'I thought your parents lived abroad, Sophy,' Nathaniel said.

'They do, but they'll be coming back to England for a few weeks leave in August. So what are you going to be doing, Marilena?'

Marilena shrugged. 'Oh, I expect it depends on Grandpa. We were going to Crete. That's where my mother spent a summer and it's why I'm called Marilena.'

Sophy picked up on this. 'Was she there with your father, d'you think?'

'She might have been. I'll never know, will I? When I'm a bit older I might decide to try to track my father down on the internet.'

'Doesn't it give his name on your birth certificate?'

Marilena glared at her friend and, intervening hastily, Nathaniel asked if they wanted more cakes. Louise wondered if Nathaniel knew the identity of Marilena's father.

As they said their goodbyes outside the school, Marilena asked, 'So what are you doing tonight, Uncle Nat? You said you had to be back in Whitchurch fairly early.'

'What?' he asked startled. 'Oh yes, a prior engagement. I'm going out to dinner.'

'I thought perhaps you and Louise . . . '

Louise coughed and saw that Nathaniel was looking amused at her discomfiture.

'I think Louise will have had enough of my company for one day,' he replied and she saw the twinkle in his eyes. 'Now, no more questions!'

★   ★   ★

On the drive back to Kent, Louise suddenly thought of Holly's party and knew she wasn't in a party mood. She had thoroughly enjoyed the day and would have liked some space to think about it. She wondered if Nathaniel was going on a date with Arlene that evening. She found the thought strangely disturbing.

Nathaniel was a good driver and stuck to the major roads whenever he could and the return journey took less time than it had on their way there, when they had taken the scenic route.

'Thanks Louise, you've been great with those girls. I've really appreciated your help.'

'They're lovely kids. I've enjoyed myself,' she assured him honestly. 'It made a total change from my usual Sunday and I'm pleased to be able to help out. The Dakars have been so kind to me.'

'They're kind people. There is just one thing though . . . ' He paused as if measuring his words. 'It might be as well if we kept today's little excursion just between ourselves and the Dakars.'

She darted a surprised glance at him. 'What about Grace?'

'I wasn't meaning Grace. She is a very discreet lady. I realise this might seem a strange request, but I have my reasons for asking . . . It's complicated.'

'OK,' she said. 'I promise I won't breathe a word.' She wondered if it had something to do with his date. Perhaps — if he was going out with Arlene — he wouldn't want her to know that he'd spent the day with Louise; innocent as it had been.

She remembered the comments Chloe and Grace had made about Nathaniel. Was there some secret — something concerning him that they didn't want her to know?

Nathaniel dropped Louise off outside Grace's house saying he'd see her on Thursday as usual. When she got inside, Grace looked a bit harassed.

'Oh, thank goodness you're back, Louise! Ryan's phoned at least three times. He was asking if you're going to that party tonight. I've been fobbing him off — told him you were out with friends and I'd no idea what time you'd be back. Very keen, isn't he? He kept asking for your mobile number, but I told him I didn't have it either. Sometimes it doesn't hurt to be a bit adventurous!'

'Thanks Grace. I suppose I'd better give him a ring now. I don't feel the least bit like going to a party but maybe I can just go for an hour or so.'

Grace gave her an old-fashioned look. 'It's none of my business, Louise, but it might be better if you let him down gently, sooner rather than later. The trouble is, you're far too nice to everyone.'

Louise smiled. 'The trouble *is*, Grace that I don't want to get seriously involved with anyone at present. I've had my fingers burnt in the past, but the occasional night out isn't going to hurt, is it?'

As she showered and prepared for the party, Louise thought about the day's events. It certainly hadn't been a date, but it had been an enjoyable interlude. The girls had been entertaining, and

Nathaniel the perfect gentleman. But his secret date got her thinking. Maybe spending the evening with Ryan wasn't such a bad idea.

5

Ryan had arranged to pick Louise up from Grace's. Holly's house was situated by the river and in a part of town Louise hadn't been to before.

'It's what people call a *town house*,' Ryan explained as he parked the car.

The noise emanating from the building was deafening. It seemed that most of the neighbours had been invited and the whole place was full of people of varying ages.

Holly came across and introduced Louise to some of her friends, several of whom she recognised from the theatre. For a time, Ryan seemed to be acting as barman. He fetched Louise a drink and then stood chatting to a group of people, replenishing their glasses.

Louise felt a bit lost. She found herself sitting with an older couple who also seemed uncomfortable in their surroundings. She couldn't help contrasting the two birthday celebrations she'd attended that day and realised it had been a strange day altogether. They chatted about general things, but it was difficult to make themselves heard over the din and so, after a bit, they gave up and sat watching the seething mass of bodies gyrating to the music.

Ryan threaded his way back to them carrying a tray of drinks. 'Great party, isn't it?'

Louise nodded and he set down the drinks and, catching her hand pulled her to her feet. As they danced, she did her best to pretend she was enjoying herself, but the room was so crowded it was claustrophobic and she found it difficult to move freely.

After several dances, Louise went in search of the bathroom. She splashed some cold water on her face, dabbed some perfume on her wrist and repaired her make-up. Suddenly, she became aware of voices drifting up from outside the open window. She didn't listen intentionally, but then she realised they were discussing Ryan and herself and her ears pricked up.

'That girl he's with tonight isn't his usual type, is she?'

There was a little laugh. 'No, he usually goes for blondes. What happened to Emily?'

'I've no idea. We'll have to ask Holly. You know Ryan. He likes to play the field — probably got tired of her. Apparently, he works with this one at the museum.'

'Does he now? It's high time he settled down. He never seems to be in a relationship for long — although he and Emily . . .'

Holly's voice cut into the conversation. 'So there you are! Whatever are the pair of you doing skulking out here? And what's that you're saying about my brother?'

Louise knew she was eavesdropping, but couldn't drag herself away as they repeated their conversation. She waited for Holly's reply.

'Oh, I'll tell you what that's all about. Ryan's fascinated by Louise because he thinks she's got a bit of a past. Apparently, she's Philip Dakar's protégée and she's very reticent about what she did before she came here. She doesn't seem to have any friends in the area either. He's like a dog with a bone — can't let go.

'She seems a decent enough sort of girl. It's about time Ryan settled down, he can't resist a challenge, can he? Anyway, when Emily comes back from the States, I'm hoping they'll get back together again. She's only got a year's contract. He was really cut up when she left.'

Louise's ears were burning. She suddenly realised that she'd got to get home. She remembered a saying of her father's, 'Forewarned is forearmed.' She grabbed her bag and made a hasty exit, nearly knocking over a girl who was waiting outside.

'Thank goodness! I thought you were taking a shower!'

Louise murmured an apology and shot down the stairs. Ryan was waiting at the bottom.

'There you are! I nearly sent out a search party. Thought you might have fallen down the plug-hole!'

Louise forced a smile. 'I was hot so I needed a wash and brush-up,' she told him, trying to sound normal.

At that moment there was a loud knock on the door and a pizza delivery man stood on the step with a stack of cardboard boxes piled up to his chin. Ryan produced a wad of notes.

'Great! Now we can eat. 'My sister's not heavily into cooking so she figured takeaways would be best. The Chinese came when you were upstairs and she's got salad stuff and other bits and pieces ... Dinner is served!' He shouted above the din.

Louise hadn't thought she would have any appetite, but when Ryan reappeared shortly afterwards, balancing loaded paper plates, she followed him outside where it was cooler and quieter by the river. He set the plates down on a wall, told her to guard them, and went off for some drinks.

The food was mouth-wateringly delicious and Louise actually found herself enjoying Ryan's company, now that she was aware that he didn't want a serious relationship, although she hadn't liked some of the comments she'd heard. She didn't want to talk about what had happened in London because it was still too painful, but it was hardly a state secret. Anyway, it seemed as if Ryan had a fairly chequered past too.

The music blared out from the open windows of Holly's town house, and there seemed to be a festive air by the river. A couple of people strolled past with a large sheepdog and called out a cheery good-evening, and some folk on the opposite bank waved.

'I like it here,' Ryan told her simply. 'OK, everyone knows everyone else's business, but so what? When I've saved enough money for a deposit, I'm aiming to get one of these town houses too. Of course, Holly only rents — as do most of the people along here.'

'So where do you live at present, Ryan?'

He looked surprised. 'Why here, of course, with Holly. I thought you knew that.'

Louise shook her head. 'No — actually, you've never said.'

He looked uncomfortable. 'Actually, I've only been here about six months. Holly's housemate moved on and mine went off to the States.'

Her head jerked up and she almost said, 'Was it Emily?' But then she realised he'd never mentioned Emily to her. Anyway, perhaps it was Emily who had joined forces with Holly's housemate! She helped herself to some more sweet and sour chicken and rice.

'Well, it obviously seems to work out OK for the pair of you — sharing, I mean.'

He nodded. 'It has its disadvantages, but we respect each other's privacy and we each have our own space. Financially it's great. Fortunately, Holly and I have always got on well together, unlike some people and their siblings. What about you?'

'Me!' Louise echoed, startled. 'How d'you mean?'

'So, have you got any brothers or sisters?'

'Just an older sister who's happily married. She lives near my parents in Yorkshire.'

'You've never really said what made you come down South.'

'I had my reasons,' she said cautiously. 'I'd always fancied working in London. It has a lot of attractions.'

'And distractions too, I should imagine,' he commented drily. 'Anyway, I assume it didn't meet up to your expectations?'

'In some ways, no. London wasn't really my scene. I'm not a city girl, but I've told you why I left. My job disappeared when the art gallery I was working in closed. It didn't work out and it proved an expensive venture, what with all the overheads.'

'And Philip Dakar appeared and conjured up a job for you in the museum. How providential!'

She shook her head. 'It wasn't like that. Actually, I approached him and it just so happened there was a temporary vacancy because Chloe was going on maternity leave. It was like the answer to a prayer.'

'Right — well, that's your story and you're sticking to it, but I strongly suspect there's a bit more to it than that — something you're not telling me. Some fellow, perhaps?'

Ryan swigged his beer. 'Ha! I'm right, aren't I!' he exclaimed triumphantly, as the tell-tale colour stained her cheeks.

'None of your business,' she retorted and stuck out her tongue playfully, trying to keep her tone light. 'Anyway, there's no mystery. I just needed a change of scenery and Whitchurch seemed the ideal answer at the time.'

They finished their food and pulling her to her feet, he caught her hand. 'Let's go for a walk by the river. Leave the plates. We'll collect them later.'

It was a beautiful evening. The moonlight reflected in the river, striking it with silver. There was an occasional splash from some small creature swimming in the water.

Several other couples were strolling along or locked in an embrace. Presently, the houses petered out. There was just a track by the side of the river bank.

Louise hesitated. 'Perhaps we ought to turn back now.'

Ryan pretended not to hear and, pulling her into the shadows caught her in his arms. 'Did I tell you, you're looking absolutely gorgeous this evening?' He ran a finger down her cheekbone, and then tilted her chin and kissed her slowly on the mouth. As he became more impassioned, she pushed him away.

'Come on, Ryan. I think you've had a bit more to drink than usual and when you sober up you're going to regret this. Now, I really ought to be making tracks. It's work tomorrow for both of us, remember.'

'You don't have to go — why don't you stay over?' he murmured against her hair. 'Some of Holly's friends will. She'll lend you a few necessary items — she always keeps a supply of spare toothbrushes etc.'

'I don't think so, Ryan — Grace would worry,' she said lamely.

'Phone her then!' he exclaimed, exasperated. 'Not that you're accountable to her. I'll drive you home first thing to change. I've got a lovely comfy, king-size bed,' he added persuasively.'

His grip tightened on her waist, but she shook her head and pulled away.

'It wouldn't make any difference if you had a four poster — the answer would still be *no*.'

'Thought you enjoyed a bit of fun,' he said crossly, but Louise ignored this and began to charge back towards the house.

'Louise — wait!' He caught up with her. 'Why are you being such a tease?'

'We hardly know each other, Ryan. I like you and enjoy your company, but

I just don't want to rush into a relationship.'

'If you say so, but that wasn't the impression I got just now,' he said gruffly.

She reached the spot on the wall where they had left their plates and scooped them up, leaving him to collect the glasses, and they went back into the house in silence.

Louise was a little concerned about the amount of drink Ryan had been putting away and realised she'd need to ring for a taxi, as there was no way she'd let him drive her home and risk being breathalysed.

The older couple, Mike and Liz, were just saying their goodbyes. Apparently, Mike's brother had come to collect them. Louise seized the opportunity and, hurrying up to them, asked if she could beg a lift.

A sullen Ryan muttered, 'It didn't have to be like this, Louise.'

Holly exchanged looks with one of her friends as Louise thanked her for the evening and followed the couple outside, drawing a breath of relief. Whatever was wrong with her? Ryan's kisses had meant nothing at all. Was it just that she was still getting over Ashley, or was it simply that — compared to Nathaniel, Ryan seemed immature?

Nathaniel had been marvellous with Marilena and Sophy. Louise had a sudden image of his laughing, amber-flecked eyes and that mop of chestnut hair.

She wasn't sure how she was going to face Ryan in the morning, but hoped that when he had sobered up, he'd see things differently. Anyway, if he had recently come out of a relationship too, he was hardly likely to want to plunge straight into another one.

* * *

Fortunately, Louise didn't run into Ryan the following day, although she saw him in the distance with a group of students. Arlene kept her incredibly busy running to and fro amongst different sections of the museum.

A showcase in the natural history gallery needed completely reorganising. A number of items had been removed and were being temporarily replaced with a collection of insects someone had brought back from their travels in the nineteenth century. They had been bequeathed to the museum by a distant relative and Louise wished they hadn't, as they were going to be fiddly to display and she wasn't keen on them.

To her surprise, Arlene sought her out during lunchbreak. She actually deigned to sit at the same table as Louise who soon discovered why.

'I'm off to London tomorrow, Louise,' she announced. 'Mr Prentice has kindly invited me to look round the museum where he's based. Anyway, there's plenty for you to be getting on with upstairs — when you've finished those displays in the natural history section.'

Arlene handed Louise a detailed

sheet which listed enough work to keep her occupied for the next fortnight, she thought grimly.

'Oh, and you needn't bother coming back here on Thursday evening. I understand how Mr Prentice works and I'm perfectly happy to be his right-hand er . . . *person*,' she laughed at her feeble attempt to make a joke.

Louise had been looking forward to Thursday evening and wondered if Nathaniel was tired of her company. She felt an inexplicable pang of disappointment. Arlene had had her hair styled differently, and Louise realised he probably preferred a more mature woman.

For once the afternoon seemed to drag. Hardly anyone came into the area where Louise was working and she was glad to get home.

'Hard day?' Grace enquired, seeing her tired face. 'I'll put the kettle on. Oh, and Nathaniel rang — wants to have a word with you. Something about visiting Philip Dakar on Wednesday afternoon.'

Louise looked at her in surprise. 'Wednesday afternoon — but I'm at work.'

'He'll explain. Give him a ring whilst I'm making the tea, dear. The number's on the pad.'

Nathaniel answered almost immediately. 'Hi, Louise. Thanks for phoning back. Would you accompany me to the hospital again on Wednesday afternoon? Philip's anxious to hear all about our visit yesterday. I've already spoken to Mary on the phone, but she says he won't be content until we've been in to see him. Can I pick you up around three?'

'I'd like to come, but I'm working,' Louise told him, her heart beating unaccountably fast.

'No it's fine; I've cleared it with the powers that be. If you're helping me out on Thursday evening, it's only fair you get some free time to make up — unless you've got another date with Ryan.'

Louise was relieved he couldn't see the hot colour rising to her cheeks. 'No,

I'm free — but I thought . . . '

'Great. I'll pick you up at around three on Wednesday then,' he said briskly, 'Bye for now.'

Louise felt bemused, thinking again that Nathaniel had been presumptuous to arrange things without consulting her first. Arlene was obviously under the impression that she'd be assisting at his lecture, as she had been the previous Thursday. Louise didn't want to cause any problem between herself and her senior. At least it solved her dilemma because, up until now, she hadn't been sure if she was expected to attend Nathaniel's lecture or not.

'Is everything alright, Louise?' Grace enquired as she came into the sitting room with the tea tray.

'Yes, fine, Grace — all sorted.'

Louise was tempted to confide in Grace about the problem she was encountering with Arlene Miles, but was determined not to burden others with her problems.

6

The following evening Louise had been invited to supper with Chloe and her husband, Steve. Chloe appeared to have got herself into a much better routine with Ava now, and the chicken dish she served was delicious.

Louise had only met Steve briefly previously. He seemed a really nice guy who insisted on loading the dishwasher and making coffee after the meal, so that the women could have a chat. However, Louise was selective about what she told her new friend; aware that Chloe would ultimately be returning to the museum where she knew everyone. Louise mentioned Ryan's party and the fact that she'd visited Philip Dakar.

'Is there any news of him coming home yet?' Chloe asked anxiously. 'I'd go to see him, but I'm not sure a hospital is the best environment for Ava.'

'Yes, perhaps it would be better for you to wait until he returns home. I get the impression it won't be too long now. Actually, I'm going to visit him again tomorrow afternoon.' Louise decided against mentioning Nathaniel or the reason for their visit.

'Oh, give him my best. He's such a nice man. I think he worries a lot about his young granddaughter . . . I suppose you know about his granddaughter?'

Louise nodded, but made no comment, intent on hearing what Chloe might have to say.

Chloe leant forward in her chair. 'Marilena's a bit of a live-wire. Mum says that's just how her mother was — spirited and full of life. You wouldn't believe it, would you? The Dakars are such quiet people.

'Of course, the Dakars consider their granddaughter as their daughter now. She's away at boarding school in Sussex. Let's hope the father doesn't surface.'

Louise stared at her. 'But I understood — I mean, someone indicated that the father's unknown.'

Chloe looked at Louise knowingly. 'If you believe that, you'll believe anything. Anyway, if the girl has a mind to, I'm sure she can find out who he is when she gets a bit older — and think of all the heartache that would cause! Now, changing the subject, tell me how you're getting on with Ryan these days. You've been to Holly's party. What next?'

'Oh, neither of us is looking for a serious relationship,' Louise assured her. 'He's good company for the occasional night out. Anyway, I gather he was involved with another girl up until fairly recently, who went to the States.'

Chloe looked relieved. 'Oh, so he told you about Emily, did he?'

'No, not exactly, someone mentioned her at Holly's party — although Ryan did say his flatmate went to the States — so I put two and two together.'

'Yes, that was Emily. She was his partner. She was offered a job over there and saw it as a career opportunity, but Ryan was opposed to her going, even though it's only for a year, initially. Anyway, I understand they had a bit of a disagreement and she went anyway.'

Chloe picked up Ava's cuddly, pink elephant, 'Ryan was so moody and miserable after she went. He really missed her in the beginning, but then he decided to stop moping and get on with life. When Holly's flatmate moved out, he moved in. Holly's another live-wire, as I expect you've realised and Ryan decided to be a bit of a man about town. Now you've come along and it's good to see the pair of you getting on so well.'

Before Louise could refute this, Steve came back into the sitting room bearing a tray of coffee and with perfect timing; Ava's whimpering could be heard over the baby monitor.

'I'll go,' Steve said. 'It's my turn. You've had her all day.'

Chloe beamed and settled more comfortably in her chair. 'Steve's devoted to Ava,' she said as he disappeared again. 'Couldn't be more supportive. Unlike some dads, who don't want anything to do with their children until they start growing up a bit.'

'The children or the dads?' Louise asked, and they creased up with laughter. There was something Louise wanted to know and, as she sipped her coffee and took the chocolate Chloe offered, she said casually, 'Last time I came round you were going to tell me something about Nathaniel Prentice, but then your mother turned up. So come on, spill. I've been wondering what you were going to say ever since.'

Chloe hesitated for a moment. 'I don't know too much — only that he and Fleur Dakar were really good friends at one point and some people think . . . '

Louise's eyes widened. 'You don't mean to say . . . ' She couldn't bring herself to put it into words, but it would make perfect sense after seeing Nathaniel with Marilena.

Chloe nodded. 'Mum once told me that there was a rumour going round a few years back, that Nathaniel was the father of the Dakar's granddaughter.'

'Then why wouldn't he admit it — accept responsibility?' Louise asked mystified. It seemed entirely out of character with the Nathaniel she was beginning to get to know.

'It's complicated.' Chloe selected another chocolate and pushed the box towards Louise. 'You see Nathaniel was going to marry Fleur Dakar. They were engaged, and then she met this other guy and ran away with him.'

Louise tried to make sense of this. 'Eloped, you mean? That sounds like something out of a Victorian melodrama. Why would she do that in this day and age?'

Chloe shrugged. 'Search me — anyway, that's what Mum told me. Apparently, when Fleur discovered she was pregnant, this other guy went ballistic — refused to accept the baby was his and sent her packing. That's as much as I know.'

Louise mulled this over. She couldn't believe that Nathaniel wouldn't be prepared to face up to his responsibilities or perhaps it was just that he didn't want to.

'But, if Nathaniel *is* the girl's father, then why wouldn't he have her live with him?'

'I suppose it would be awkward; his work often takes him abroad. Amongst other things he's an archaeologist, you know. He lectures all over the place and takes part in digs — very hands on. It would be difficult with a child in tow.'

'But she's at boarding school. No there has to be more to it than that!' Louise exclaimed and then, seeing Chloe's curious expression, stammered, 'I — I mean it's probably as you say — just a rumour. I mean there are such things as DNA tests, aren't there?'

'Yes, but they're not compulsory,' Chloe pointed out.

Just then Steve came into the room carrying Ava. 'This little lady is wide awake and wants to know what's going on down here!'

'Steve you know what I said about us making a rod for our own backs, if we keep on bringing her down here. She'll never want to settle down to sleep and then we'll have a problem when she gets older, but I suppose we could always make an exception.'

Chloe gave a broad grin and, taking the baby from her husband, cradled her in her arms. Ava gave a tiny sigh and promptly fell asleep. It was a perfect scene of domestic bliss and Louise was reluctant to leave, but knew the following day was going to be busy.

* * *

Louise had scarcely set eyes on Ryan since Sunday, but he suddenly appeared in the gift shop as she was waiting for her colleague, Katarina, to relieve her so that she could meet up with Nathaniel.

'Louise, I haven't had a chance to meet up with you since Sunday . . . '

She finished serving a customer. 'That's OK. It's been manic,' she said reasonably.

'I was off in London visiting the

museum where Nathaniel's working, yesterday.'

She stared at him. 'You went as well as Arlene?'

He grinned. 'Yes, I think she got a bit of a surprise when I turned up at the station. She thought the invitation was meant exclusively for her. As I've said before, she seems to have got a bit of a crush on Nathaniel Prentice.'

So that explained Arlene's less than sunny mood that morning and the rather curt reply Louise had received when she'd enquired if Arlene had enjoyed her day at the other museum.

Ryan leant across the counter. 'Look, Louise, I want to apologise for Sunday. I realise now I was too full on.'

'There's really nothing to apologise for,' Louise said airily. 'It was a good party and maybe you'd had a little too much to drink, but you were mostly good company. Let's forget about it, shall we?'

Ryan looked relieved. 'Does that mean you're prepared to go out with me again?'

There was no-one else in the shop and he took her hand and gazed earnestly into her eyes. 'If I promise to take things more slowly, how about us going to the cinema or having a meal at that new Mexican place in the market square?'

Louise smiled. 'I'd like that Ryan.' He had the sort of persuasive charm that Ashley had had, but she was aware of it, and wouldn't let him sweet talk her into doing anything she didn't want to do. She had absolutely no intention of becoming too involved with Ryan Clarke.

There was a slight cough. Startled, Louise looked up, thinking it was another customer, but to her embarrassment, she saw it was Nathaniel Prentice.

'I hope I'm not interrupting anything. Time's ticking on, so if you're ready, Louise . . . '

Louise felt the tell-tale colour stain her cheeks. 'No — yes, I mean I'm just waiting for Katarina to relieve me.'

'I think she's on an errand for

Arlene,' Ryan informed her.

'Right — then I'm sure you wouldn't mind covering for a few minutes, Ryan, as you seem to be at a loose end,' Nathaniel said crisply.

Ryan looked as if he were about to protest, but then thought better of it and meekly went to stand behind the counter. Louise hurriedly dashed off to collect her jacket and tidy herself up, wishing Nathaniel had not arrived at that precise moment.

Nathaniel was waiting in his Jaguar looking impatient. Louise was glad she had come on the bus that morning, so that she wouldn't have the problem of picking up her car later.

'Sorry to have kept you waiting,' she murmured.

'Not at all. I'm the one who should be apologising for interrupting the pair of you just now. It would be as well, however if, in future, you kept your private life separate from your work.'

'That's what I endeavour to do,' Louise said sharply. 'Anyway, what business is it of yours?'

'None whatsoever,' Nathaniel replied mildly, his brown eyes sparking with amber lights, and he turned on the ignition.

'It was hardly my fault if Ryan came to speak to me just now,' she said in clipped tones.

'And I'm sure he's regretting it at this very moment,' Nathaniel told her, a slight smile playing about his lips. 'I don't imagine working in the shop is his forte.'

Louise saw the glint in his eyes. She was tempted to say that Arlene had known she needed to leave sharp at three, and had deliberately prevented Katarina from relieving her on time.

Fortunately, Nathaniel turned the conversation to other matters. Louise was initially fuming that Ryan should have placed her in such an awkward position but realised that she went along with him and it wasn't his fault.

When they arrived at the hospital, they found Philip Dakar looking much more like his old self. He was reading a weighty tome on Egyptology.

'Ah — hello. It's good of you to come. I'm in danger of dying of boredom, just as I'm recovering from my other ailments.'

'Don't listen to a word he says,' Mary cautioned them. The worried lines had left her face, and it was apparent that her husband was well on the way to recovery.

'Tell us about Marilena, and then Louise and Mary can go for a coffee whilst you and I discuss your forthcoming lecture, Nat.'

Nathaniel looked amused. 'OK, you're obviously going to keep me on my toes, so it's a good job I've come prepared with some notes. Anyway, first things first. The visit on Sunday went well, didn't it, Louise?'

They told the Dakars most of what had taken place, although Louise noticed that Nathaniel made no reference whatsoever to the problems they'd encountered at the outset concerning the girls' maths class.

'And did Marilena mention Fleur?' Philip wanted to know.

'No more than usual,' Nathaniel replied carefully.

Louise saw the look that Mary shot her husband and how she quickly changed the subject, and realised she didn't want to discuss this in front of Louise.

'Are you able to help out with Nat's lecture tomorrow, Louise?' Philip asked her. 'Arlene called in to see me last Friday and gave me a blow by blow account of her part in the previous evening's proceedings.'

'I'm available to help this week — if Nathaniel needs me,' she added hastily.

'That's good,' Philip nodded. 'Arlene said how much she was looking forward to her trip to London, Nat. How did it go?'

'Absolutely splendidly. Ryan Clarke came as well. You know how keen he is on the Celts and we've got a marvellous exhibition at present.'

Ten minutes later, Louise and Mary left the pair of them together deep in discussion.

'There's something I feel I must

tell you,' Mary said, as they sat over coffee and biscuits in the hospital cafeteria.

Louise looked at her enquiringly.

Mary sighed. 'Now that you've met Marilena, I think it's time I filled you in with some of our family history, before someone else does. I asked Nat to leave it to me. You may have heard about our daughter, Fleur?'

'I know she sadly died,' Louise said cautiously.

Mary took a sip of coffee. 'She was our only child and very bright. After a gap year, she went off to university and we were as proud as punch. At that time, Nathaniel was working at the Whitchurch museum. He showed great promise. He was a few years older than Fleur, but they got on so well, and when they decided to become engaged, we were really pleased.

'Anyway, during the summer vacation — after her second year at university, Fleur went to a music festival with some of her student friends and she met a man there who completely captivated her. She broke things off with Nat and told us she was going to Crete with this man to visit his grandmother — who had rented a villa out there for the summer. And that was just the beginning . . . '

Mary paused to sip her tea, visibly upset, and Louise waited, wondering what she was about to hear.

'When Fleur came home, she had changed,' Mary continued quietly. 'It was as if this fellow had brainwashed her. She announced she'd become engaged to him and was wearing a flashy ring to prove it. And then she informed us she'd got no intention of returning to university. Apparently, life had far too much to offer to spend it on studying. She was returning to Crete.'

She paused again, screwing her handkerchief into a ball. 'I'm afraid we had a dreadful row and she just flounced off. It was the last time I saw her alive.'

Mary dabbed her eyes and Louise patted her hand, not sure what to say.

'Marilena is so much like her mother.

I couldn't bear it if she were to go the same way. I know we mustn't be too protective but . . . '

'Marilena seems a sensible girl,' Louise said comfortingly, hoping she would be forgiven for being a little economical with the truth.

'There are so many temptations out there. Of course, once this man — I can't even bring myself to say his name — once he discovered Fleur was pregnant that was it, as far as he was concerned. Apparently, he didn't want children and refused to accept that the baby was his.'

Louise was anxious to hear the rest of the story. 'But obviously your daughter was convinced he was the father, wasn't she?' She waited with bated breath.

'Yes, but this is where it gets difficult. When Fleur returned from Crete the first time, she went to say a final goodbye to Nat, and was foolish enough to tell her fiancé she'd done so. She sowed the seeds of doubt in his mind; so that when he found out she was pregnant, he wouldn't accept the child was his. It broke Fleur's heart when he said he wanted nothing more to do with her.'

'So how did you find all this out?' Louise prompted. 'Did she get back in touch?'

Mary shook her head. 'No, but Elinor — the grandmother did. She phoned from Crete to tell us her grandson and Fleur had had an argument and parted company, but didn't give us any details at that time. She said Fleur was safe and she'd taken her under her wing.'

'That was kind.'

Mary nodded. 'She was the only member of the family who showed any compassion towards our daughter. She phoned again a few weeks later — this time to tell us that she'd returned to England and Fleur was staying with her, but still didn't want to see us. That's when we learnt the truth and found out she was pregnant. Elinor said she was sure, given time, Fleur would come round. She just needed to think things through.'

'So did you have the grandmother's address?'

'No, but Elinor kept in touch for some while after that. She was convinced that her grandson was the father of Fleur's baby, and assured us that our daughter was being taken care of, and that she would make sure she was provided for. And then suddenly all went silent. Sadly we didn't hear from her again.'

'So what happened to Fleur after that?' Louise asked gently.

Mary shook her head. 'We've tried to piece it together, but we're not really sure. We think she either went to a woman's refuge or a commune for a short while. If only she'd contacted us we would have supported her, but she didn't get in touch.'

Mary's voice broke. 'When someone finally rang her father, Marilena had already been born and Fleur was in a dreadful state and in need of medical attention. By the time Philip got her to the hospital it was too late to save her.'

'That is so very sad,' Louise said, feeling the tears springing to her eyes. 'Thank you for confiding in me.'

Mary blew her nose. 'I'm afraid there's more. 'We'd found a letter from the grandmother amongst Fleur's things, mentioning a diamond and emerald necklace. Elinor stated that she'd originally gifted it to Fleur to wear on her wedding day. Elinor went on to say that she now intended Fleur to keep it as a legacy for her child.'

Louise's eyes widened. 'So did you find this necklace?'

Mary shook her head. 'Sadly, no. A short time after Fleur died, Elinor's grandson turned up at the museum looking for Nathaniel. There was an ugly scene. It was dreadful. You may have noticed the scar on Nat's chin?'

Louise's stared at her. 'That man attacked him?'

'I'm afraid so. Naturally Nathaniel tried to defend himself. Poor Nat was accused of all sorts of things. Elinor had died suddenly from a heart attack, and the family were accusing Fleur of stealing a valuable heirloom.

'In her letter, Elinor stated that she'd sent a copy of the letter to her solicitor, and also that she'd mentioned the necklace in her new will. Unfortunately, her executors have denied all knowledge of both the original letter and any new will. Our solicitor sent them a copy of the letter but, to this day we don't know what became of the jewellery. If and when it turns up then, hopefully, it's legally Marilena's.'

Mary managed a little smile. Anyway, enough of that! We're blessed with Marilena. Without her our lives would be empty. You might wonder how we could bear to send her away to boarding school. We thought it would be for the best, because she'd get to mix with other girls of her own age, whereas round here, there aren't so many and, with us being older than the average parents, she might miss out socially.'

'But about the family of this other man?' Louise pressed, her mind racing on. 'Didn't they want to know about their granddaughter?'

Mary shook her head again. 'They were so callous. We contacted them to inform them what had happened to Fleur and told them about her baby. We pleaded with them to talk with their son — get him to show some compassion and take some responsibility for Marilena — have a paternity test. We had a curt reply from their solicitor saying that the family believed their son when he said he wasn't the father, and mentioned the missing heirloom again.'

'That's appalling! So, forgive me for saying this, but I suppose there's still an element of doubt as to who Marilena's biological father is?' Louise held her breath.

'We only know what Fleur told Elinor.' Mary reached for her handbag and took out her powder compact. 'And, of course, what Elinor said in her letter. That's how we knew how to contact the family . . . I'm sorry, my dear, I've spent far too long talking about our family problems, but you have a sympathetic ear. Come on — let's go back to Philip and Nathaniel.'

7

'Things seem to be looking up, don't they?' Nathaniel said on the way home. 'I thought Philip seemed a great deal brighter today, didn't you?'

'Yes, much more his old self. Mrs Dakar seemed a great deal happier about him too. These past weeks must have been a real strain for her.'

'The Dakars really appreciated us taking the girls out on Sunday but, I thought it best not mention what Marilena had said about their holiday on Crete. She's so set her heart on going but I honestly can't imagine Philip being given the OK to go gallivanting quite so soon after his heart problem.

'It's such a pity. Isn't there anyone else at all who could take her?' Louise asked. Crete is such a beautiful island.'

'Have you been there?' he asked, shooting her a glance.

'No, but I've read about it. I had hoped to go, but it didn't work out.'

She and Ashley had talked about spending the summer there, but then their relationship fell apart. He'd probably gone with the red-haired Erin instead, she thought bitterly.

'It gets mighty hot during the summer months,' Nathaniel remarked. 'Easter's the nicest time, but the Dakars couldn't make it then and so it looks like Marilena's going to have to wait a bit longer. And no, sadly, there isn't anyone else to take her.'

As he dropped her off at Grace's he said, 'I'll see you presently — unless you're out with Ryan this evening.'

Louise stared at him, mystified. 'No, not tonight — but what do you mean? Have I forgotten something?'

He laughed. 'Perhaps you've chosen to put it out of your mind. Grace has asked my mother and me to supper tonight, and I'm sure the invitation includes you — unless you've made other plans, of course.'

Louise's heart missed a beat as she wondered why Grace hadn't mentioned it to her. Thanking Nathaniel for the afternoon, she scrambled out of his car and dashed into the house.

'Grace, I didn't realise you'd got company tonight. You should have told me. Look, I'll lend a hand and then I'll make myself scarce.'

Grace shook her head, blue eyes twinkling. 'You'll do no such thing! I knew you'd say that, which is why I didn't mention it sooner. Now there's plenty of time. Everything's under control. I'm doing a straight forward chicken dish and I've cheated with the dessert — doctored a bought one with more fruit and cream. If you can just set the table and find the wine glasses, then you can go and get yourself changed. You can tell me all about your visit to see Philip Dakar.'

On occasion, Grace treated her like her mother might have done, Louise reflected with a rueful smile as she shook out the tablecloth.

She had a quick shower and changed into a pale pink skirt and a floral top; applying light make-up and leaving her shining, dark hair swinging loose about her shoulders.

After her brush with Nathaniel earlier that afternoon, Louise felt a little apprehensive about spending the evening with him, but at the same time, she felt a surge of pleasure at the thought of being in his company again so soon.

'So is Mrs Prentice staying with Nathaniel at his friend's cottage?' she asked presently, as she hunted out the pastry forks.

'Yes. It's all worked out rather well. Celeste's been dividing her time between Nathaniel and his sister whilst she's been having some renovations done on the house. She's a lovely lady, but can be a little overpowering. Anyway, it's the only opportunity I've had to ask her for a meal and, as you've already met her, I thought you'd like to see her again.'

To Louise's relief the evening went

well. Nathaniel was at his most charming and so attentive towards his mother and Grace that Louise saw yet another facet of his character.

She looked at him across the table now. He looked relaxed, and as if he liked nothing better than spending his evening with the two older ladies and her. His dark chestnut hair fell forward over his forehead and his dark brown eyes were full of interest. Her heart lurched as he met her gaze and treated her to one of his devastating smiles. She felt a wave of emotion as she noticed the scar on his chin. The Dakars obviously didn't believe he was Marilena's father — even though they probably wished he were. She felt sure that he would have accepted responsibility if that were so.

For a time the conversation centred on general topics and then, naturally it turned to their visit to the hospital that afternoon.

'I really must go to see Philip before I return home,' Celeste said, helping herself to more vegetables. 'The problem is, I hate hospitals.'

'I don't think anyone is exactly enamoured with them — unless they work there,' Grace commented drily. 'Look, why don't you and I pop in for half an hour or so tomorrow afternoon?'

'Ye-es, I suppose that would be ok, although I have to get back pretty sharpish. I'm cooking an early meal because Nathaniel's got his lecture tomorrow evening and he's invited that very nice young woman, Arlene Miles, who works at the museum to eat with us, and then she's accompanying me to his lecture.'

So that was how Nathaniel was working it to appease Arlene. Louise did not look at him. She felt a sharp pang of something akin to jealousy.

'Louise has kindly consented to being my assistant again. I'll be talking about the Saxons.'

'Good, I'm looking forward to it,' she told him with forced cheerfulness. She was obviously useful to him — if nothing else. 'I'm sorry I missed your last lecture, though because I'm fascinated by the Romans — they were so civilized.'

'Do you really think so?' Celeste shuddered. 'They might have been advanced when it came to heating their houses and taking baths, but they were so cruel. No, they're not really my cup of tea at all.'

Nathaniel winked at Louise. 'You'd have missed your tea, Mother, wouldn't you, if you'd lived in Roman times,' he said gravely.

And everyone laughed. 'Of course, Kent is riddled with Roman sites such as — Dover, Canterbury and Lullingstone,' Grace commented.

'Yes, indeed. Perhaps I can take you to Lullingstone one day, Louise. We can take a look at the Roman villa.'

'That would be interesting,' she said feeling slightly amused; she hadn't been asked on a date to view a Roman Villa before!

★   ★   ★

When the meal was over, Louise got to her feet and offered to make the coffee. To her embarrassment, Nathaniel followed her into the kitchen with some empty dishes. Whilst Grace was an extremely good cook, she did tend to make rather a lot of washing-up and there was no dishwasher. Louise began to gather up the dirty crockery.

'Don't worry, I'm used to Grace's kitchen,' Nathaniel told her, as if he could read her mind. 'Let's do the washing-up. Those two are so deep in conversation they won't even notice we're missing — I'll wash and you dry.'

Louise laughed. 'That's what Grace always says.'

'Ah well, that's who I caught it from!' Seeing her look at his attire he smiled and removed his jacket, carefully draping it over the back of the kitchen chair. Louise picked up a tray and went to clear the rest of the dining room table. When she returned, he had filled the washing-up bowl with hot soapy water and gave her a boyish smile.

'I'm in a bit of a predicament!' He held out soapy hands and she realised the cuffs of his crisp white shirt were still fastened with gold links.

As she obligingly removed them for him and rolled up his sleeves, she realised that being in such close proximity to him was having a strange effect on her pulse. She caught the fresh, tangy fragrance of his cologne and looked at his strong wrists and hands, and a little shiver trembled along her spine.

He placed a soapy finger on her lips. 'Thank you, Miss Gresham — now I can do my job so much better.'

'I'll put your cufflinks here in the pot on the dresser, along with your watch,' she told him, trying to regain composure. 'You've used half a container of washing up liquid!'

He chuckled. 'That's half the fun, surely?' He cupped his hands and blew a bubble which floated towards her. She blew it back and it burst just as it reached him. They dissolved into laughter.

They finished the washing-up in record

time, after that. As Louise put the things away and attended to the coffee, Nathaniel said, 'This job of yours at the museum, Louise, isn't entirely to your liking, is it?'

She turned to look at him in surprise. 'What makes you say that?'

He dried his hands and rolled down his sleeves commenting, 'I get the impression that it doesn't exactly stimulate you'

She stared at him. 'Has Dr Dakar said anything?'

He shook his head. 'No, of course not, but I'm fully aware of just how capable you are, and would think you're over-qualified for the job you're doing. It must be frustrating for you to be a kind of glorified dogsbody.'

'Chloe didn't seem to mind,' she said, wondering what he was driving at.

'Chloe is in rather a different position from you, I would imagine. Besides, I think you've taken on a slightly different role. From what I've observed, you seem to have been put upon on occasion.'

'Oh, I don't mind,' she said, trying to sound casual. 'It's a job, and I'm on a learning curve. I've never worked in a museum before and it's providing good experience for me.'

He retrieved his cufflinks and stood in front of her fastening his cuffs and she had a sudden urge to reach out and touch him.

'So what are your plans for when you leave Whitchurch?' he asked casually.

'I'll worry about that when the time comes,' she told him sharply, realising it wasn't the first time he'd mentioned it. 'Now we'd better drink this coffee before it gets cold.'

Louise didn't have time to puzzle over his questions, however, because just then Grace came into the kitchen and stood there arms akimbo.

'So this is what the pair of you have been up to! My guests are barred from the kitchen, Nat, but I have to say the pair of you have done a splendid job. Mind you, a body could die of thirst if they were waiting for you to make them a drink, Louise!'

'But you'll enjoy it all the more, now you haven't got to think about the washing-up,' Nathaniel pointed out with a grin.

She smiled back at him. 'Your mother and I have already made inroads into those chocolates you brought, so you'd better hurry up before all your favourites get eaten.'

For the remainder of the evening they had a hilarious game of Scrabble, which both Grace and Celeste were addicted to. It was almost eleven o'clock before they left.

'Such a delightful young man,' Grace commented, as she packed away the Scrabble. 'Celeste is blessed with her children.'

'Grace, I know about those rumours concerning Nathaniel and Dr Dakar's daughter — surely there isn't any truth in them?' Louise asked tentatively.

Grace stopped to retrieve a letter T from beneath the coffee table. 'There's always gossip,' she said carefully. 'If you mean, is there any truth in the rumour that Nathaniel and Fleur Dakar were engaged at one time then, yes, they were. But, if you've heard other speculation — then it's just that — speculation. Let's leave it at that, shall we? It was a long time ago and a lot of water's flowed under the bridge since then. There's been a lot of heartache. Sometimes it's best to just leave things be.'

'Yes, I'm sorry. I didn't mean to be inquisitive,' Louise said awkwardly.

Grace placed a hand on her shoulder. 'It broke the Dakar's heart when Fleur died so soon after Marilena was born. She neglected herself, you see. By the time Fleur asked for help, it was too late. Anyway, Marilena is the light of their life now and, to be honest, I think they prefer to believe they are her parents, even though they are really her grandparents.'

Louise nodded. There were further questions she wanted to ask, but she knew that Grace wouldn't be prepared to answer them, so she had to be content with what Mary had already told her. She supposed Nathaniel and Fleur Dakar must have been quite young when they were engaged. What a tragedy that Fleur had met this other man who had ruined both their lives!

★   ★   ★

The following day, Louise was kept busy as usual. During her lunch break she did a mountain of photocopying for Nathaniel's lecture, and stowed it away carefully in his tray in the office.

She had been looking forward to seeing Nathaniel again, but when she did, he was cool and professional and seemed rather preoccupied. She set out the room for his lecture, according to his instructions, and pinned charts and maps on the wall. Finally, she helped him arrange a series of Saxon artefacts on a couple of tables.

Arlene breezed in just as they were on the last lap. 'Everything to your satisfaction?' she enquired of Nathaniel.

'Absolutely! So, if you're ready,

Arlene, we'd better get off. Can I leave you to finish off here, Louise? I'll see you back here around seven.'

Louise nodded and, shortly afterwards, having collected all the handouts and placed them neatly on his desk, locked the room carefully behind her and went out to her car.

★ ★ ★

There seemed to be more people than ever at the lecture that evening, and the first part of Nathaniel's lecture accompanied by illustrations of some of the prominent Saxon sites in Kent and other parts of the country went exceptionally well.

After this, Nathaniel said they'd take a look at the handouts, and then break for coffee before having a more detailed look at the artefacts he'd brought along for them to see. They would be using the worksheets he had provided for reference, and there was also a questionnaire.

Louise handed out the first page of the worksheet, but then realised that the second sheet was obviously the previous weeks', as it was about the Romans. She had a quick word with Nathaniel who frowned and looked at his master copies.

'However could that have happened? They must have got mixed up and yet . . . ' He referred to his file.

'I'm sure I checked them,' Louise said, miserably aware that it had been down to her to have spotted the glitch earlier.

'I'm afraid we seem to have a slight problem with the worksheets, ladies and gentleman. If you can just bear with me for a few moments, we'll get it sorted out during the coffee break,' Nathaniel told them in his calm voice, but Louise could tell that he was irritated.

Arlene sprang to her feet. 'I'll go and get the rest of the copies done now,' she told him. She smiled all round and, whisking up Nathaniel's copy sailed from the room — the very model of efficiency. Louise hadn't got the remotest idea of how the mistake could have occurred. She always checked and double checked, but something had gone inexplicably wrong and she felt responsible.

'It's ok,' Nathaniel reassured her in an undertone. 'Photocopiers are notoriously awkward beasts at the best of times. Perhaps one of last week's sheets got in with the others. Anyway, it just so happens I've got a short film for just such an eventuality, on an archaeological dig I was involved with a couple of months back.'

Within a matter of minutes, the audience were watching the film and Louise sank onto a chair feeling humiliated.

Arlene returned with the correct handouts, making Louise a little suspicious. The photocopier had odd quirks and wasn't the speediest of models. Before long the lights were back on and they were trouping out to coffee.

'So, what happened to you?' Arlene asked Louise. 'That really was an inexcusable mistake. Don't you ever look at what you're copying?'

Louise opened her mouth to retort, but Ryan catching up with them, and obviously overhearing the remark, put his arm protectively through hers.

'If you care to remember, Arlene, Louise wasn't around for last week's lecture, so even if she was responsible for the error, it was hardly her fault. After all, someone must have given her last week's handout to copy. Anyway, there's no damage done, is there? Everyone obviously enjoyed that film and it's created a talking point over coffee.'

A slight colour tinged Arlene's cheeks and she said softly, 'The problem with you, Ryan, is that you're biased. Mind you, had it been your lecture that had been mucked up, you may not have been so charitable!' And she flounced off to catch up with Celeste and Nathaniel.

'You want to watch your back, Louise. For some reason Arlene's got it in for you,' Ryan murmured. 'Now, whilst I've got you to myself for a few minutes, how d'you fancy seeing a Kate Winslet film — one of the ones she got the Bafta award for?'

Ryan screwed his face up comically as he tried to remember the title, making Louise laugh, and immediately, she felt the tension leaving her.

'Whatever it is, I'm sure I'll enjoy it. When and where?' Assuming that's an invitation?'

'Certainly is — Saturday night at the Community Centre our way — begins at eight. The local Film Society's showing it again by popular demand. Pity I can't remember the title! I know we're both working, but if we both went for a Mexican at that place in the High Street, I've told you about, we could still make it by seven forty five. I'll get the tickets in advance.'

'You're on,' she said. 'A little light relief is just what I need.'

Fortunately, and much to Louise's relief, the rest of that evening went without a hitch, and judging by the applause at the end, everyone had enjoyed Nathaniel's lecture.

'That went well,' Grace enthused, as

Louise drove her home afterwards. 'You mean — apart from the muddle over the photocopies,' Louise said miserably.

'I wouldn't be at all surprised if someone mixed them up for you,' Grace commented. 'I know you well enough by now to realise how meticulous you are about checking and rechecking.'

Louise had to admit that the thought had crossed her mind. 'But who and why? I mean the whole thing is so petty, isn't it?'

'That tall blonde woman who was sitting with Celeste — just tell me how she redid all that photocopying in such a short space of time?'

Louise shot Grace a look. 'That was Arlene Miles — you mean you think she was responsible for mixing the papers up? Ryan did warn me about her.'

Grace nodded. 'You'll never prove it, of course, but I saw the expression on her face.

'But why?' Louise asked in bewilderment. 'I mean why on earth would she do such a thing?'

'I can think of any number of reasons why she'd want to discredit you. You're young, bright and pretty *and* you've captured Nathaniel's interest. She's just plain jealous.'

Louise felt the colour flooding her cheeks. She shook her head. 'I find that difficult to believe. Arlene's got a lot going for her and she seems to get on really well with Nathaniel.'

'The trouble with you, Louise, is that you're lacking in self-confidence. You need to believe in yourself.'

Louise knew Grace was right. Ashley had been a strong character and somehow, after that episode in her life had closed, she had begun to doubt herself. Well it was time she turned over a new leaf and changed her image.

*   *   *

Fortunately, the following day, Louise had been assigned to the education room where she was kept so busy with several parties of school children that she didn't have time to worry about Arlene.

On Saturday, she helped out with a family workshop until four-thirty that afternoon. After tidying the room, she flew home to shower and change for her date with Ryan. To her surprise she thoroughly enjoyed the evening. The Mexican food was good and the film, *The Reader*, excellent.

Ryan was on his best behaviour. He placed a hand over hers during the performance which she didn't object to, and gave her a gentle kiss at the end of the evening.

'Thanks Ryan, I've thoroughly enjoyed myself,' she told him sincerely.

'Enough to come out with me again sometime?' he murmured against her hair.

'Yes, of course, I enjoy your company,' she told him sincerely, but she realised she'd need to make it clear that she didn't want anything more than friendship. She didn't have any romantic feelings for him and — in all probability — Emily would be coming back into his life at some point in the future.

★　★　★

On Sunday evening she had just washed and dried her hair and was doing some ironing in the kitchen when there was a ring on the doorbell. She hastily switched off the iron and went to see who it was. To her surprise and secret delight, Nathaniel stood on the step clutching a book.

'My mother's sent this for Grace. May I come in?'

'Well yes, she's at the evening service, but she'll be back shortly. I'll make some coffee.'

She ushered him into the sitting room and, trying to compose herself, went back to the kitchen, switched on the kettle for the coffee and finished ironing her blouse.

A few moments later Nathaniel came into the kitchen. 'Actually, I wanted to ask you another favour,' he told her and stood leaning against the door jamb.

'Can it wait until I've finished this or I won't have anything ironed to wear tomorrow.'

'Ok. Shall I make the coffee?'

Louise nodded and concentrated on the blouse, wondering whatever he wanted, and feeling ridiculously uncomfortable at his nearness in the confines of the small kitchen. She hung up the blouse and folded up the ironing board. Nathaniel took it from her.

'Where does it live?'

She opened the cupboard door and he popped it in with a flourish, deftly catching the feather duster which bounced out as it frequently did. They laughed.

'I'm beginning to think this kitchen is like an assault course.' He reached out and caught a strand of her hair between his fingers. 'I like your hair loose like that. It suits you.'

Her heart pounded wildly and she busied herself laying the tray and finding some biscuits. 'So — what's this favour — another trip to Brighton?' she asked when she could trust herself to speak.

He chuckled. 'You're on the right lines. It's Marilena's school's speech day next Saturday — or whatever they call these occasions nowadays. Anyway, Mary Dakar thinks Philip's likely to be discharged soon, and needs to be around for him, so she's asked if I could manage to go instead and, with a little reshuffling, I can just about fit it in and so I was wondering . . . '

'If I'd come with you?' Louise finished for him, her pulse racing. 'I would have thought that after the mess up I made on Thursday, you'd have been only too pleased to dispense with my services.'

'Don't be daft — you undervalue yourself, Louise.'

She blushed and then, seeing his amused expression said hastily, 'I take it that was what you were going to ask me, wasn't it?'

'Yes, but there's actually a bit more to it than that. You see the Dakars usually stay overnight in a hotel so that that they can take Marilena and Sophy out for lunch on Sunday.'

Louise was taken aback She was unprepared for this. 'Oh, I see. Right — that's a bit different, isn't it? I mean I'm not sure . . . '

She felt herself colouring again, as she met his steady gaze. His brown eyes seemed to spark dangerously with amber lights.

'I can assure you, I'd be on my best behaviour,' he said stiffly. 'You don't need to worry about your reputation or believe everything you hear about me, you know. Anyway, think it over. If you don't want to accompany me, just let me know, and I'll get out my little black book and choose someone else!'

Plonking the cafetiere on the tray he marched off with it, leaving Louise staring after him, miserably realising she'd handled the situation wrongly and offended him. She knew she was attracted to him, but things were moving too fast. When and if she entered into another relationship, she was determined to take things more slowly. She would never again allow herself to be ruled by her heart.

The sound of Grace's key in the lock sent her scurrying into the hall.

Grace chattered away like the proverbial magpie as usual, but Louise was uncomfortably aware that Nathaniel, whilst replying pleasantly to his hostess, addressed very few remarks to her.

When Nathaniel had gone, Louise collected up the empty cups and saucers, sensing that Grace would say something.

'Have you two had words?' Grace asked, not being one to beat about the bush.

'Whatever makes you think that?'

'Nothing much gets past me. I picked up the vibes between you, and I'm not too keen on bad feeling in my house.'

Louise stammered, 'It's not — I mean. Look, it was just a stupid misunderstanding!'

Grace sniffed disapprovingly. 'Well, if I were you, I'd sort it out. Nathaniel's a lovely chap and perfectly reasonable,'

She said no more and, still smarting, Louise went into the kitchen to wash up. Everyone kept telling her what a lovely fellow Nathaniel was and she wanted to believe this, but there was just a little element of doubt at the back of her mind. She had been used once by an unscrupulous man who had been a smooth con-artist, and she had no intention of allowing herself to get into that situation ever again.

8

'You're looking very serious this morning' Ryan told Louise the following morning as she encountered him in the photocopying room. 'What's wrong?'

'Absolutely nothing. I'm just a bit preoccupied, that's all.'

She tried to edge past him to get to a cupboard, but his hand shot out and caught her sleeve.

'Have dinner with me tonight, that'll cheer you up. I could do with your company. I had a horrendous time yesterday — obligatory family function. My brother and I don't get on and we had words.'

'I see, so you want me to be a good listener so that you can offload all your problems onto me. So, how exactly is that going to cheer me up?'

Ryan looked suitably chastened. 'No, that wasn't fair, was it?'

Louise shook her head. 'Anyway, I'm afraid I can't manage tonight, I've a hundred and one things to do, so thanks, but no thanks — on this occasion.'

'Lunch then — in our usual little place.' He was very persistent.

'I've got a stack of work to do, today, Ryan.'

'So have I, but we'll both work better on a full stomach.'

Louise capitulated. 'Oh, all right then, but I must get on now. Arlene's on the warpath.'

'All the more reason to escape for a short while. Can you manage one o'clock?'

She nodded. He was irrepressible, but she'd have to be careful not to let anything slide about the following weekend.

Louise couldn't find what she was looking for in the cupboard and bent down to rummage around in the large drawer at the bottom. 'Arlene said there's a box of leaflets and postcards around here somewhere, but I can't find them.'

Ryan stooped to see if he could lend a hand.

'Louise, what on earth are you doing?'

Arlene's shrill voice made them both shoot up so suddenly that they bumped into one another, and stood there laughing helplessly.

Arlene was not amused. 'When the pair of you have quite finished larking about, perhaps you'd care to remember that we're due to open to the public in precisely five minutes!'

Louise avoided Ryan's gaze. Arlene was becoming more like a stern school teacher every day.

'You asked me to locate those leaflets and postcards that are needed in the upstairs gallery,' she reminded Arlene.

'Oh, yes, well I've found them now. They were in a box on the window sill all the time. You obviously didn't look beyond the end of your nose. Now, Louise, you're going to have to manage on your own for a while because I've got a meeting with Mr Tomlinson.'

Arlene paused, her hand on the door frame. 'By the way, Nathaniel Prentice rang up just now to say he won't be able to give the lecture this Thursday, after all. It seems he's double-booked.'

There was a sinking feeling in Louise's stomach.

'So the evening's been cancelled?'

Arlene raised her thinly pencilled eyebrows sharply. 'Not at all; apparently, we've got an archivist coming. It promises to be a very interesting talk. She's bringing her own assistant with her, so you won't be needed this week — unless you want to come as a member of the audience.'

She swept out of the room.

'I don't know what's got into Arlene recently,' Ryan murmured. 'She didn't used to be so hoity-toity.'

Louise didn't comment. So far as she was concerned, Arlene had never been any different. She hurriedly closed the drawer and raced upstairs to the gallery just as the first members of the public arrived.

Louise didn't have time to brood because it was a particularly hectic morning, but as she grabbed her jacket and raced off to meet up with Ryan for lunch, she wondered what on earth she could do to put matters right between herself and Nathaniel. Surely he hadn't taken umbrage just because she hadn't immediately jumped at the opportunity of spending the weekend with him?

She had to admit to herself that the very thought of spending that amount of time in Nathaniel's company made her go weak at the knees. She suddenly felt selfish as she thought of Marilena. After all, the poor girl needed someone there to support her. Louise realised she'd have to think things through carefully and fast.

Ryan was impatiently waiting for her, as she hurried down the stairs.

'Come on — let's escape quickly before there are any more delays! Arlene wasn't the only one to get dragged into that meeting this morning! Talk about doom and gloom! It looks as if we're going to be facing cutbacks like everyone else in the recession. I just hope it doesn't mean any job losses.'

Louise felt a sinking feeling in the pit of her stomach and it wasn't hunger. She'd known from the word go that she was only employed in Whitchurch on a temporary basis, but she really liked living in Kent and was beginning to settle down. The months were slipping away and she couldn't bring herself to start job hunting — not just yet. Louise had hoped that, if she proved her worth, there might be another job opportunity when this contract ended. She'd wondered if perhaps Chloe wouldn't want to return when her maternity leave was up.

She sighed. The problem was that Arlene seemed intent on finding fault, and would rarely let her use her own initiative. Not only that, but her emotions were in turmoil and she realised that, against her better judgement, she was beginning to think about Nathaniel Prentice far too much.

'You look as if you've got all the troubles of the world on your shoulders today,' Ryan told her, as they sat at a table in the sunny little courtyard surrounded by bright tubs of flowers and hanging baskets.

'Perhaps I have,' she agreed gloomily. 'Anyway, leave me out of it for the moment. What's the problem between you and your brother?'

Ryan gave a little laugh. 'Oh, just the usual sibling rivalry, I suppose. Tim has always been the apple of my father's eye. He's bright, good-looking, got the *Midas* touch — everything he touches turns to gold and he's got a lovely wife and family.'

'And you're just plain jealous,' Louise told him candidly.

'What?' He frowned and she waited for him to react but, fortunately, their order arrived just then. 'Ok,' he conceded. 'But that doesn't prevent me from thinking that he's a big-headed, bumptious, self-righteous . . . Why are you laughing?'

'Oh, Ryan, if you could only see the expression on your face! And do stop waving that fork around. All brothers and sisters fall out sometimes; it goes with the territory — but I'm sure you must have something in common.'

'Oh yeah,' he agreed reluctantly, 'we both like cricket.'

'So there you are then. What did you fall out about yesterday — or shouldn't I ask?'

Ryan looked embarrassed. 'Tim thinks I'm sponging off Holly. He says it's high time I got a place of my own.'

'And is he right?'

Ryan looked even more uncomfortable. 'In some ways, yes, I suppose so. Oh I pay my way, but it's not that simple. I'm still paying off my university loan and sometimes Holly subsidises me by letting me off one or two bills. I'm not terribly good at managing money — so now you know!'

'Well, we can't be good at everything, can we,' Louise said reasonably. 'But you're not going to tell me you're a pauper, Ryan. You must earn a good salary. At Holly's party you told me you were saving for a deposit — was that just a pipe dream?'

He nodded. 'I suppose I'm just a bit extravagant — like the good life and use my credit card too much.'

'So, at the end of the day, your brother is only pointing this out for your own good,' Louise told him firmly.

Ryan pulled a face. *'Don't you go all holier than thou on me, too!'*

'If you didn't want my opinion, why did you tell me?' she asked severely.

'You sound just like Arlene! Working with her is obviously rubbing off on you.'

They finished their meal practically in silence and, as they drank a quick coffee, Ryan asked rather sullenly, 'Ok, so what would you do, if you were in my shoes?'

Louise considered. 'Sit down with Holly and have a rational discussion about the housekeeping, for one thing. You obviously need to cutback — change your spending habits. I'll pay for lunch — no arguments!' She snatched up the bill and got to her feet.

'I'm sorry, I haven't even asked you what's been troubling you,' Ryan said as they made their way back to the museum.

'It'll keep,' Louise said shortly. There was no way she wanted to discuss her present dilemma with Ryan. She could just imagine what his reaction would be.

* * *

When Louise arrived back at Grace's that evening she found Mary Dakar there.

'Louise, I've dropped by, in the hopes I'd catch you, and Grace has kindly asked me to stay for supper. Have you had a chance to speak with Nathaniel about this weekend yet?'

Louise was aware that Grace was listening intently as she laid the table. 'Yes, he did mention it yesterday,' she said carefully.

'Oh, dear, this is a bit awkward,

Louise. Philip's likely to be discharged in the next day or two, so I've realised there's absolutely no question of my going to Marilena's open day — much as I'd like to. The problem is, Philip's fretting about it. I know it's a lot to ask, but Marilena seems to have taken to you and we'd so appreciate it if . . . '

Louise didn't know what to say. She caught Grace's eye.

'But you see, I'm not one hundred per cent certain if I can get the time off, Mary.'

Mary Dakar's face creased into a frown. 'Oh, dear, what a pity! I'll have to get back to Miss Shawcross soon.'

'Miss Shawcross? Is that one of Marilena's teachers?' Louise asked, puzzled.

'Goodness no! Didn't Nat explain? Harriet Shawcross is Sophy's aunt — or rather her great-aunt. She's a delightful lady, but rather old-fashioned. We usually meet up for lunch on these occasions. Anyway, when I spoke to her originally on the phone, she invited me to stay with her, instead of in our usual hotel. I phoned her again to explain that Nat's offered to go in my place, and she was wondering if you could come too.'

Grace had gone into the kitchen. Louise had never felt so embarrassed in her life. 'Oh, I see — I thought . . . Oh, gosh!'

Mary looked mystified. 'So obviously Nat didn't explain any of this, did he?'

Louise shook her head and managed a weak smile. 'I'm afraid it's probably my fault — I didn't really give him a chance. You see he mentioned that you and Dr Dakar usually stayed in a hotel and . . . '

'And you thought . . . ' Mary clapped her hand to her mouth and Louise saw the twinkle in her eyes and coloured. 'Oh, Louise, I can see how it must have appeared to you!'

Mary lowered her voice. 'But Nat would never take advantage of the situation. He's a lovely person.'

'So everyone keeps telling me.'

Louise dearly wanted to add, '*but*

I've heard a rumour that he's been a bit of a womaniser in the past.' She had thought Ashley was a lovely person too, when she'd first met him, but now she knew differently.

'I suppose you haven't told Nathaniel about the bad experience you had before you came here?' Mary asked, as if reading Louise's thoughts.

'No, I'm trying to move on — put it all behind me. I'm sorry, Mary, I've made a bit of a fool of myself, haven't I? And now Nathaniel's away until the end of the week and I don't know how to get in touch with him.'

Mary's face cleared. 'But I do — so, does that mean you'll reconsider?'

Louise made her mind up suddenly. 'Yes, providing I can get the time off. I'd enjoy seeing the girls again *and* meeting Sophy's aunt.'

'Actually, she's her great-aunt. I'm warning you she's quite a character, a stickler for etiquette — one of the old school!'

Grace bustled into the room with a

loaded tray. 'All sorted?' she enquired.

'More or less,' Mary told her. 'Nathaniel's gone off on one of his archaeological digs with a group of students until the end of the week. Apparently, it had totally slipped his mind, but fortunately I've got his mobile number, although he's probably down a ditch somewhere. Now Louise, we'll just need to sort out your work commitments.'

'I might be able to swap with someone,' Louise put in hastily, 'although it's a bit short notice.'

'Come and have your supper for now and then Mary can phone Nat from here.'

Over supper, Mary told Louise a bit about Harriet Shawcross. Apparently, when she was a girl, she had attended the same school as Sophy and Marilena. She loved having the girls to visit, but found them a bit boisterous, which was why the Dakars usually ended up taking the pair of them out on the Sunday afternoon, after they'd all had lunch together.

After supper, Mary phoned Nathaniel.

After a moment or two she passed the phone to Louise. To her relief he sounded his normal friendly self.

'Hi Louise. So are we all set for the weekend?'

'Providing I can get the time off.'

'That won't be a problem — leave it with me. I'll sort it out and get back to you soon. Got to go now, I'm taking a lecture in ten minutes. And thanks, Louise. I know Philip and Mary will really appreciate this.'

Louise felt that the situation had been taken out of her hands. She didn't know what to expect from the forthcoming weekend and wished she could go back to the previous evening and start all over again.

* * *

'For a newcomer you certainly manage to work the system,' Arlene told her irritably on Tuesday, as they did some running repairs to one of the wall displays.

165

'How d'you mean?' Louise stared at Arlene, trying to think what she might have done to annoy her now.

Arlene applied the staple gun fiercely to some backing material.

'Most of us have a strict rota where Saturdays are concerned, but you seem to get them off to order. There are things that I'd like to do, too. Still, we can't all have friends in high places!'

'Polly is keen to do the overtime. She's got a heavy mortgage,' Louise said defensively.

'That's as maybe,' Arlene sniffed, 'but she doesn't often work up here, so she doesn't know the ropes.'

'I'm sure you'll find her equally as efficient as I am,' Louise retorted, tongue in cheek.

'I'm afraid that's not saying a great deal, is it? We wouldn't be doing this display if you'd secured it properly the first time round, would we?'

Louise smarted. 'That school party were rather undisciplined,' she pointed out. 'I've found chewing gum on the bench and someone's pencilled obscenities on a couple of the posters!'

Arlene pursed her lips and stepped back to examine her handiwork.

'That'll have to do or neither of us will get any lunch break. Let's hope there'll be no more mishaps. You're wanted downstairs this afternoon, Louise . . . So where is it you're swanning off to on Saturday?'

'I'm job hunting,' Louise told her and marched off to the other end of the gallery before Arlene realised she was winding her up.'

'You think you're so clever, don't you?' Arlene said standing with her hands on her hips, as Louise gathered up some empty crisp packets.

Louise didn't reply, which only served to make Arlene more infuriated than ever.

'Perhaps I ought to remind you that this job is only temporary. When Chloe returns you'll be out on your ear and so — if you know what's good for you — you'd better watch your step. You'll need me to give a reference when you actually are job hunting again.'

Louise didn't think this spiteful comment was worthy of a reply. She dropped the crisp packets into the waste paper bin, and had stooped to retrieve a pencil from beneath a bench when a piercing screech brought her to her feet.

Arlene was standing rigid, her face as white as a sheet. Louise rushed to her side. There in the centre of one of the displays was one of the biggest spiders Louise had ever seen.

'Goodness what a specimen! Shall I call Peter? He might want to have it for his collection,' Louise said more calmly than she felt. Ryan poked his head round the door.

'Whatever's the matter? I thought someone was being murdered.'

'Arlene's discovered a rather large arachnid,' Louise told him.

Ryan took a look and roared with laughter. 'Yes, you should definitely ask our Keeper of Natural History, to take a look at that, Arlene!'

Stretching over, he picked up the spider by its legs. 'It's one of those dreadful plastic things! Some child playing a joke, I suspect. He'll probably come and ask for it back tomorrow.'

Arlene, who was perched on the edge of a chair, looked sheepish.

'Why don't you go to lunch?' Louise suggested, suppressing a strong desire to shriek with mirth. 'You look as if you could do with a strong coffee.'

Without another word Arlene got to her feet and swept out of the room.

'Oh, dear,' I suppose I'll get the blame for that as well,' Louise said, straightening a pile of worksheets.

Ryan deposited the spider in a convenient pot. 'You mean she'll accuse you of planting it there to make her scream blue murder?'

'Something like that. Whatever I do, I seem to rub her up the wrong way.'

'Don't let it get to you,' he advised. 'You got off to a bad start so far as she was concerned.'

'How d'you mean?' Louise demanded.

Ryan hesitated. 'I shouldn't be telling you this, but Arlene had Chloe's job all lined up for a cousin of hers, and then you appeared on the scene — so she wasn't best pleased.'

Louise whistled. 'So she's been harbouring a grudge all this time. Well, that explains a lot — are you sure that's all there is to it?'

'Isn't that enough? You're popular with everyone else and you're good at your job. Arlene was hoping you'd be incompetent so that she could replace you with her cousin.'

Louise swallowed. 'So far as Arlene's concerned I *am* incompetent! It's hardly my fault, is it? I mean I didn't know about the cousin. I don't intentionally do things to annoy Arlene, whatever she may think!'

'Of course you don't,' Ryan said soothingly. 'How about coming out for a meal on Saturday night? And there's this jazz concert on in town that I'm keen on going to — a mate of mine's got some spare tickets.'

'Sorry Ryan, I'm away this weekend.'

He looked disappointed. 'Pity — are you doing anything special?'

'Just visiting friends,' Louise said carefully. She didn't like being deceitful, but knew that she needed to be discreet. She still felt a bit unsure about the weekend, and went hot when she thought of her last encounter with Nathaniel. It was such a shame, because now they would be like strangers again.

9

Louise was pleased to learn that Philip Dakar had been discharged from hospital on Wednesday. She felt obliged to go to the archivist's talk the following evening. It was interesting, but didn't hold her attention as Nathaniel's lecture would have done.

Friday arrived at last. Louise was in a quandary as to what to wear for her weekend away. She had just spread several outfits on her bed when there was a tap on the door and Mary Dakar popped her head round.

'I hope you don't mind, Louise, but Grace said you were busy packing and I've brought a few things for you to give to Marilena. My neighbour's keeping Philip company for a while. They're having a game of chess — not my scene at all.'

Louise invited her in. 'It's good to

know he's back home . . . Actually, I'd be grateful for your opinion because I'm not sure what to wear tomorrow,' she said worriedly.

'Well, let's see now — that black and white dress is nice. How about teaming it with this red jacket?'

'Won't it be too bright?'

'Not at all — it's very fashionable.'

Louise felt relieved. 'I won't need a hat, will I? Or a fascinator?'

Mary laughed. 'Good gracious no! It's not compulsory. It's not as if you're going to Ascot.'

Louise couldn't resist a smile. 'I told Arlene I was job hunting! I'm afraid I was being a bit bad!'

Mary chuckled when Louise explained. 'Poor Arlene, I'm afraid she doesn't have much of a sense of humour. Now, let's take a look at what else you've got to wear. You'll need something comfortable to travel in — and then there's Sunday lunch to consider. I'm not sure where Nathaniel's taking you all, but it's bound to be somewhere smart.'

It was soon sorted and then Mary sat in the armchair and explained about the things she'd bought for Marilena. Grace brought up a tray of coffee and some fruit cake and they all sat chatting.

Louise mentioned it was her father's birthday and how she'd phoned him up just before he'd gone out for a family meal.

'I expect your family miss you, don't they Louise?' Grace asked.

'Yes, and I miss them too, but I speak to them regularly on the phone, as you know.'

'If any of your family decides to visit they're welcome to stay here,' Grace offered for the umpteenth time.

'Thanks Grace — I've already told them that. They only want what's best for me and would never stand in my way. Anyway, it's not as if it's forever — I mean I've only got a very temporary job at the museum.'

'But wouldn't you like to stay on — if you were given the opportunity?' Mary enquired. 'You've fitted in very well — so they tell me.'

'I really enjoy working there but, unfortunately, I seem to rub Arlene up the wrong way,' Louise said ruefully, thinking about what Ryan had told her.

Mary set down her cup and saucer. 'Arlene eats, breathes and sleeps the museum — even if she pretends otherwise. It's her life. She was married briefly, but it ended on a sour note when her husband left her for someone else. From what I can make out, she now has quite a difficult home life. She lives with her mother who's a semi invalid and is both possessive and domineering. As you grow older, you'll realise it's important to try to understand what makes a person behave as they do.'

It was a gentle reprimand and Louise nodded and bit her lip. Mary was a kind and wise person and always saw the best in everyone. Scooping up the clothes from her bed, Louise hung them up ready to pack in the morning.

'Have you shown Mary that photograph of your little nephew?' Grace asked, to cover an awkward moment.

Louise passed it to Mary. 'My sister says he's growing up so fast that I won't recognise him next time I see him. He's almost three now.'

'They're gorgeous at that age. I remember Marilena — naughty with it, of course. Speaking of photographs, Grace, I was wondering if we could take a look at the album again. I'd like to show Louise the photographs of Fleur.'

Grace nodded. 'Of course, you can. I'd like to see them again, myself. I'll just fetch the key.' And she disappeared from the room.

'Grace keeps it here for us until Marilena's older,' Mary explained, indicating a small locked cupboard on the wall. Louise had often wondered what it contained but hadn't liked to ask.

'Of course, Marilena's seen a number of photographs of her mother — but these are special — mainly of Fleur and Nathaniel. You see we've never told her that they were once engaged. We've been waiting for the right time. She's very fond of Nathaniel, but, at the moment, she's still immature emotionally, and we don't want to give her any ideas. Nathaniel's not her biological father — more's the pity,' she added wistfully. 'Things would have been so very different for all of us if he were.'

Grace returned with the key. 'Nathaniel's left a few of his things here,' she explained to Louise. 'I expect you wondered what was in this cupboard.'

Louise nodded. 'But won't he mind us looking?'

'Bless you, no. I've asked him about them often enough. Mostly it's just sport's trophies, books — that sort of thing. Apart from the album, which he's keeping for Marilena until she's older and more able to understand what happened.'

Opening the cupboard, Grace extracted a red, leather-bound album. The three of them sat on Louise's bed poring over the photographs. Louise looked at pictures of a younger Nathaniel, his arm entwined through a lovely young woman's. Fleur was so like Marilena that it took Louise's breath away.

There were photographs of Fleur and Nathaniel in the Dakar's garden or on various outings, and others of Fleur on her own. Louise felt a lump in her throat as she gazed at them. It was all too obvious that Nathaniel had idolised Fleur and she looked so happy. Why then had she let herself be lured away by this other man?

After a while, Mary Dakar snapped the album shut with a sigh. 'So, you see, it just wasn't meant to be,' she said quietly. 'We can't possibly know why life deals us these cruel blows, I suppose.'

Louise, who had been wondering that herself, made no comment.

'Maybe it's just as well we can't,' Grace said, removing the album from her friend's lap, and carefully replacing it in the cupboard on top of a pile of books. As she did so, a silky, rainbow-coloured scarf fluttered down from the shelf.

'Well, will you just look at that!' Mary exclaimed. She picked it up and smoothed it out. 'Now that's something Marilena might like to have. I remember the birthday when Nat gave it to Fleur. He said it matched her every mood. She used to tie her hair back with it. It made her look rather bohemian. She had such beautiful hair, thick and the colour of honey — like Marilena's. Do you think you could put it in your bag, Louise? Tell her we've come across it at the back of a cupboard. Did you see Fleur wearing it in the photo taken when she was on that picnic?'

Louise nodded. 'She looked lovely,' she told her friend, sincerely.

'It's just a pity we can't come across that necklace so easily,' Mary added sadly.

Grace gave her a questioning look and Mary said, 'It's all right, I've told Louise about it. Of course, Philip and I aren't so naïve that we haven't realised it could have been lost or stolen, but we still live in hope that it might turn up one day. After all, it is supposed to be Marilena's inheritance.'

Mary smiled, but inwardly she was worried. She and Philip hadn't intended to throw Louise and Nathaniel together. It had just happened, but if their relationship was to develop into anything other than friendship then there might be a problem. After all, there were certain issues to be dealt with first. Things of which both Mary and Philip were certain the pair of them were unaware.

★　★　★

Louise was up and about early the following morning, not wanting to keep Nathaniel waiting. She dressed in a pair of neat green trousers and a multi-coloured top and caught her hair back in a ponytail. Nathaniel turned up at nine o'clock sharp and they left almost immediately.

'Harriet Shawcross is expecting us for a light lunch around midday so woe betide us if we're late.'

They drove for part of the way in silence, and then Nathaniel told her about his time at the archaeological dig, and how they'd unearthed some Saxon relics — obviously another ancient burial site.

'We didn't find anything of great significance, but the students were happy enough. It's great to see such enthusiasm from young people. Now, I'm going to pull in for coffee shortly — there's a rather nice pub just along here.'

'I'd like to get a gift for Miss Shawcross,' Louise told him, but I don't know what to buy.

'Ah, now I've had a thought about that. Supposing we get her some flowers and then treat her to lunch tomorrow?'

'Seems like a good idea to me.'

As they relaxed over coffee in the pub's attractive garden, Nathaniel turned to Louise. 'I'm sorry I didn't explain more clearly about the arrangements for this weekend.'

She coloured, wondering what Mary Dakar had said to him.

'It's ok, you just took me by surprise that's all,' she murmured, feeling foolish. 'It was good of Miss Shawcross to invite us to stay.'

Nathaniel's dark eyes glinted with amusement. 'There's certainly not likely to be any hanky-panky under her roof. She's a very correct sort of lady!'

This remark only served to make Louise blush even more furiously. She decided it was a good job he couldn't feel her heart racing.

★   ★   ★

Harriet Shawcross turned out to be a lady of indeterminate age with beautifully styled grey hair, a lovely complexion and a ramrod-straight, back. She lived in a picturesque, chocolate box cottage with a wealth of pink roses scrambling up the walls. Louise was enchanted.

They sat in the comfortable dining room eating salad and cold meats and discussing the state of affairs in the country.

'So, Louise — what brought you to the south of England?' Harriet asked suddenly, and once again, Louise found herself explaining how she'd fancied a change of scenery.

Harriet Shawcross gave her a keen look. 'And are you settled in Whitchurch?'

Louise was aware that Nathaniel was listening to her every word. 'For the time being,' she replied briefly. 'I like Kent and what I've seen of Sussex so far.'

Fortunately Harriet caught sight of the time at that point and, after Louise had helped her to clear away, Harriet ushered her guest upstairs into a beautifully furnished bedroom to get changed.

Some cottage, Louise thought appreciatively as she freshened up in the en-suite shower room. A fluffy black cat sat on the window seat surveying Louise with large yellow eyes, as she got dressed.

'So, do you approve?' Louise asked, tickling the cat under the chin; it purred loudly.

When she went back downstairs,

Nathaniel was waiting in the sitting room reading a copy of *Country Life*. He was looking incredibly handsome in his pale grey suit. She noticed that he had added a blue silk tie to his immaculate white shirt.

'Will I do?' she asked, giving him a twirl.

'You look enchanting,' Nathaniel told her softly and, getting to his feet, put a hand lightly on her shoulder, making her heart leap. But then she remembered the way he had been looking at Fleur in those photographs, and wondered if he would ever be able to give his heart to anyone else again.

The afternoon provided a different experience for Louise. Although the school had been greatly modernised, it was still quite formal. After the speeches and prize-giving, came a delightful musical entertainment by the choir, of which both Marilena and Sophy were members.

After this, the girls marched them off to meet their form teacher and to show them various pieces of their work. As they were making their way to the art room, Harriet Shawcross stopped to speak to Miss Hardy, and a large lady wearing a rather bright floral two piece, accosted Nathaniel.

'Hi! It's Nathaniel Prentice, isn't it?' she asked in a marked American accent.

Nathaniel inclined his head, as she peered at him from beneath the brim of an amazing hat. So much for no hats, thought Louise, amused.

'We met last year on that dig in Suffolk. I'd just come along to take some photographs.' She nodded towards Louise. 'Is this your wife? So nice to meet you.' And before either of them could reply, she'd moved off.

Nathaniel raised his eyebrows and grinned. 'D'you suppose Marilena's married us off?' he asked, sotto voce, barely concealing his amusement.

'If she has then we're going to have to tell her we've got divorced!' Louise rejoined in the same light-hearted manner.

'And I was just getting used to the idea,' he bantered, his eyes dancing with merriment. He linked an arm through hers. 'Come on — let's go and socialise.'

Harriet Shawcross was still engaged in conversation with Miss Hardy, and the two girls were hovering impatiently nearby. Marilena suddenly darted across to Nathaniel and Louise.

'Whoever was that lady talking to you?' she wanted to know.

'Do you know, I haven't got the remotest idea — I was hoping you could tell me? I'll give you a clue. She's decidedly American.'

Marilena screwed up her face in thought. 'Oh, I expect that'll be Letitia Marlon's aunt by marriage . . . Actually, Miss Hardy would like a word with you, Uncle Nat, and I haven't done anything bad, I promise.'

Louise left Nathaniel to talk to Miss Hardy and sat on a convenient chair looking out over beautifully manicured lawns and neatly tended flower beds.

For a moment or two she allowed her thoughts to drift, wondering what it would be like to be married to Nathaniel, and what sort of a husband he would make.

Louise was aware he could be kind and considerate, but he also had very definite views on things and obviously enjoyed taking charge of situations; which was hardly surprising considering the nature of his job. He had a great sense of humour too, and she admired his sharp intellect.

She looked in Nathaniel's direction now, as he spoke with the headmistress, and a little shiver ran down her spine. Overshadowing everything, even after all these years, was his deep love for Fleur Dakar. Louise could tell, just by looking at the photographs Mary had shown her the previous evening, that Nathaniel had adored Fleur. Would he ever be able to love anyone in that way again?

'Louise!'

Louise came to with a start to find Marilena standing beside her.

'Sorry, Marilena, I was miles away looking at those beautiful grounds. Did you want to show me your artwork or shall we wait for Nathaniel?'

'He'll know where to find us — come on.'

She marched Louise along a maze of corridors to the art room where she pointed out several of her paintings 'My mother liked art. I've got a couple of her sketch books back at my grandparents' house. I think I'd like to go to Art College when I leave school.'

'Really? You've certainly got talent, but surely you don't need to decide quite yet. Have you discussed this with your grandparents?'

'No, but I do need to think about my options, don't I? So what do you think Miss Hardy wants with Uncle Nat? She's been talking to him for ages.'

'I'm afraid I've got absolutely no idea, but I expect he'll tell you,' Louise assured her.

Shortly afterwards, Nathaniel joined them, but he didn't enlighten them;

instead he studied Marilena's pictures, a thoughtful expression on his face.

'I particularly like that one, Marilena. Where is it?'

'Crete. I looked at lots of travel books and brochures and then I closed my eyes and imagined I was there. I painted it from my imagination.'

Louise studied the vividly coloured painting, and felt a pang of empathy towards the young girl. Marilena so badly wanted to go to Crete — to follow in her mother's footsteps — it had almost become an obsession.

After a delicious tea, they wandered round the grounds and then Nathaniel retrieved the box of goodies Mary Dakar had sent for Marilena from his car. Louise had put the other things into a hessian shopping bag of Grace's, and now she popped them into the top of the box. After making arrangements to collect the girls at around twelve thirty the following day, the adults departed.

Harriet Shawcross served up a

beautifully presented evening meal, but the portions were so dainty that Louise thought Nathaniel would be starving hungry before breakfast. She watched him help himself to several crackers and a large chunk of cheese after his rather meagre bowl of fruit salad and cream.

To Louise's surprise, Harriet proved to be quite a wizard at Scrabble and the rest of the evening passed by pleasantly.

10

It seemed to Louise that her head had barely touched the pillow when she was awakened by the sound of thunder. She lay there for a few moments, too comfortable to move, but then as the storm grew closer, she went to look out of the window, just in time to see the heavens open. She stood there watching for a while and was just about to scramble back into bed again when she heard the sound of voices coming from the landing. Shrugging on her housecoat, she flung open the door. A black shadow hurled itself at her and she shrieked.

'Louise, whatever's wrong! Are you hurt?' came Nathaniel's concerned voice.

'No, no. It's just Harriet's cat. He startled me!'

'Oh, poor Dusty! He must be

terrified!' cried Harriet.

Louise ventured onto the landing, wondering what on earth was going on. Nathaniel, dressed in a fetching silk-satin dressing gown, was looking upwards whilst Harriet was wringing her hands in dismay. A steady trickle of water was coming through the ceiling.

'The builder was supposed to be coming to take a look next month. I was hoping it'd be all right until then,' Harriet wailed.

Nathaniel sprang into action and began to roll up the lovely Chinese rugs. 'Not to worry. It was obviously a flash flood. Where can I put these Harriet, so that we don't trip over them?'

Harriet opened the door of a tiny box room and he carted the rugs inside and draped them over a pile of cardboard boxes.

'Louise do you think you could go with Harriet and find a bucket to catch the water in?' he called from the doorway. 'It's practically stopped raining so, hopefully, it won't be too bad.'

Louise followed Harriet into the utility room and hurried back upstairs with a large galvanised bucket, a mop and a pile of newspapers. She couldn't help smiling when she saw that Nathaniel had rolled up his pyjama trousers and kicked off his slippers as if he was prepared to paddle.

'What's so funny?' he demanded. 'If you're grinning at the sight of my legs just wait until you see me in my shorts!'

He mopped vigorously and Louise laid down the newspaper. When they had finished their tasks he wrung out the mop and then, catching hold of it, suddenly fell backwards making Louise laugh.

'If I had any breath left, I'd sing that song my mother likes from the seventies, *Raindrops keep falling on my head*,' Nathaniel whispered.

'Is everything all right up there?' enquired Harriet Shawcross, coming to the foot of the stairs.

'Absolutely,' Nathaniel reassured her. 'We've nearly finished.'

'Only I've made you some tea and toast.'

They sat round the large pine kitchen table munching toast and marmalade and, before long, it had stopped raining and a watery sun broke through. The birds were singing merrily.

'Well, what a night!' Harriet said, pulling her quilted dressing gown more securely about her. 'I dread to think how I'd have coped if the two of you hadn't been here. I'll have to get on to the builder at the earliest opportunity.'

'If I were you, I'd phone your insurance company as well,' Nathaniel advised her, reaching for another slice of toast.

It was almost six o'clock when they got up from the table.

'I'm never going to sleep now,' Louise said, pushing back her tousled hair. 'You know I'd really like to get dressed and go for a walk.'

'Good idea, I'll join you,' Nathaniel told her, thinking how pretty she was looking — so natural; her hair in a soft dark cloud about her shoulders. Just for a moment, he considered how pleasant it would be to look at her across the breakfast table every morning.

'But it'll be so wet underfoot and the fields will be muddy,' Harriet pointed out.

They assured her they'd be fine and off they set. It was already turning into a clear, bright morning. Louise breathed in the rain washed air appreciatively.

As Harriet had forecast, it was quite wet and muddy along the lane bordering the cottage, but it didn't deter the pair of them,

'D'you think there'll be any more breakfast when we get back?' Nathaniel enquired. 'I think I could eat a horse.'

'I've got a packet of biscuits in my room,' Louise told him. 'I brought them for the journey in case we got stuck in a traffic jam.'

'This is turning out to be a strange weekend. Do you suppose Harriet is watching us from the window?'

'Possibly, why?'

He flung a casual arm about her shoulder. 'Because I'd like to thank you for coming with me, and to apologise for any misunderstandings there might have been between us.'

They had reached the end of the lane and there was a gate leading into a meadow full of poppies and oxeye daisies. Nathaniel pulled Louise gently to him and kissed her lightly on the mouth.

'Friends again?'

She nodded, unable to speak in case she betrayed her feelings for him. The kiss had awakened desire within her, but she was determined not to show it.

When they arrived back at the cottage, Harriet was in the kitchen making porridge. There was an appetising smell of frying bacon.

'I thought you might be hungry after your walk and I always have something cooked for Sunday breakfast.'

They accompanied Harriet to church, which was half a mile down a twisting lane. Louise shared a hymn book with Nathaniel who sang in his rich honeyed voice. The sun shone through the stained glass windows, casting rainbow patterns and making it impossible to believe the mayhem the storm had caused during the night.

'I would have liked to have stayed on for coffee,' Harriet said wistfully after the service. 'The builder and his wife are here today and I really do need to have a word with him about my roof.'

'Is there any way you can get someone to give you a lift home?' asked Nathaniel. 'We can go on ahead and pick up the girls, and fetch you from your cottage on the way back.'

Harriet seemed quite agreeable to this arrangement and so Nathaniel and Louise drove the short distance to the school to collect Sophy and Marilena.

Seeing their outfits, Louise explained that they'd need to bring a change of clothes with them because Nathaniel was planning to take them bowling that afternoon.

'Aunt Harriet will never agree to that,' Sophy said dismally.

'I'm sure she will — just leave it to me,' Nathaniel assured her and winked.

Lunch was an unexpected delight, in an old farmhouse which had been turned into a restaurant. The girls behaved impeccably and the meal was a great success — a traditional roast with all the trimmings, followed by a selection of mouth-watering desserts.

Harriet Shawcross seemed to have enjoyed herself but, as they sat over coffee on comfortable sofas in the oak-beamed lounge, she suddenly looked tired and Louise realised that the lack of sleep was obviously catching up on the elderly lady.

'Time we were making a move, I think,' Nathaniel said briskly, exchanging a knowing glance with Louise.

'Now Harriet, I was wondering if you'd prefer a nice, quiet afternoon at home whilst we take these young ladies off your hands for a couple of hours or so?'

'Oh, but I couldn't expect . . . I mean you've done enough already. Wouldn't you prefer to come back to the cottage?

Sophy and Marilena can go in the garden.'

The girls looked downcast.

'I tell you what,' Nathaniel suggested. 'Supposing we bring them back to you for half an hour so after our outing, before returning them to school? How would that be?'

To everyone's amazement, Harriet agreed. Louise decided that Nathaniel was an expert at getting his own way, although perhaps that wasn't strictly fair. After all, he had to have good organisational skills in order to do the job that he did.

Once back at the cottage, the girls grabbed their sports bags and rushed indoors to change. Louise followed at a more leisurely pace.

Harriet raised her eyebrows when her niece and Marilena reappeared dressed in jeans and T-shirts.

'We don't want to spoil our best clothes, Aunt Harriet,' Sophy informed her solemnly.

Harriet stood at the cottage door

waving them off; Dusty weaving about her legs.

'I hope you two still want to go bowling — otherwise I'm stumped for an idea,' Nathaniel told them as he pulled out of the drive.

'Definitely!' they chorused.

It was another fun-packed afternoon. Louise couldn't help comparing Nathaniel with Ashley. Ashley would have been in his element taking her to some flashy event in his sports car. So far as he was concerned, the more miles they covered in a day and money he spent the better. Spending an afternoon going bowling with two young teenagers would have been far too tame for him.

All too soon it was time for the girls to return to the cottage where, after tea and biscuits, they got changed again, collected their things and said their goodbyes to Harriet. To Louise's surprise, Harriet had baked a cake for the girls to share and gave them each ten pounds spending money.

Nathaniel had decided it would make

sense if he and Louise drove straight back to Whitchurch after dropping Marilena and Sophy off at their school. Harriet had looked a little disappointed.

'Do come and see me again, won't you? I do so hope all that business with the roof hasn't put you off.'

'Not at all,' Nathaniel assured her. 'We like a bit of an adventure, don't we, Louise?'

'Absolutely,' Louise agreed. 'We've had a lovely time.'

After they'd thanked Harriet for her hospitality, they all piled into Nathaniel's car. In no time at all, they had delivered the girls back to school, said another round of goodbyes, and were homeward bound.

'Well, that was different,' Nathaniel commented. 'I have to say that — in spite of a few glitches — I enjoyed myself. Thanks for your company, Louise. I think Harriet genuinely meant what she said about us visiting her again.'

'I think she's a lovely lady — even though she is a bit set in her ways. She must get lonely living on her own.'

'I expect she does. All the more reason to pay her a visit when we're in the area . . . ' Before he drove off he said, 'Now, you're probably wondering what Miss Hardy had to say to me yesterday afternoon?'

Louise had been curious as to what they'd been talking about, but didn't like to admit it and so she merely smiled and looked at him questioningly.

'It seems that Philip's promised to give a lecture at Marilena's school before the end of term. It's obviously slipped his memory and, of course, there's no question of him doing it now. Amelia Hardy hadn't realised he'd been so ill.

'Anyway she's asked if I'd be prepared to step in. I've made a provisional arrangement, but I haven't mentioned it to Marilena yet, because I'll need to check my diary — make sure I haven't double-booked myself — before finalising the details. Also I realise Marilena's concerned about her grandfather, so I don't want to draw her attention to the fact that he's still not fit enough to work.

'Louise, I know it's a big ask but Marilena's taken to you so would you be prepared to come with me on that occasion too?'

'I'd love to unless — what about Mary Dakar?'

Nathaniel shook his head. 'I honestly can't see that happening just yet with Philip still recuperating. Now, I realise you'll need to sort out your off-duty, so if you just pencil in the date provisionally for now and then I'll get back to you as soon as possible.'

Louise carefully wrote the suggested date in her diary and decided she'd better book it out anyway.

'Now the second thing Miss Hardy wanted to see me about was to tell me that Marilena's still convinced she'll be going to Crete in the summer holidays. She just can't seem to get it into her head that it's not going to happen, and she's been overheard telling her friends about it.'

'Oh dear, that's difficult,' Louise sympathised. 'And there really is no prospect of anyone else accompanying her?'

Nathaniel concentrated on his driving and did not reply for a moment or two. 'I've been thinking about it long and hard,' he said at last, 'but I honestly don't think it's a good idea for me to take her myself. It's a difficult situation for the Dakars. I'm afraid Marilena's got a fixation about Crete at present, as you saw from that painting. She's so anxious to see the villa where her mother stayed, and to find out if anyone remembers her. Whilst we feel sure it would help her to get it out of her system, there is, of course, one big problem.'

'What's that?' prompted Louise.

'At present we don't want Marilena to know the identity of her real father or she might try to seek him out. That could be disastrous if he rejected her — as we feel sure he would. If that's what she's got in mind, then it's going to need some very careful handling. The

Dakars haven't even told her about her great grandmother, or mentioned the missing necklace which is supposed to be Marilena's inheritance . . . It's ok, Mary told me she'd explained to you about that.'

Louise nodded. 'Mmm. I can see that it's a delicate situation. So why did the Dakars tell her about her mother going to Crete in the first place?'

He sighed. 'They didn't want Marilena growing up without knowing anything about either of her parents. They've always wanted her to know as much as possible about Fleur, but I suppose as Marilena's got older she's been asking more direct questions. The Dakars aren't prepared to tell her the circumstances of her birth until she's more grown-up, but they're pretty certain Crete's where she was conceived and she knows that — so you can understand why she wants to see the place for herself?'

'Yes, it's quite a poser, isn't it? Poor Marilena,' Louise sighed sympathetically.

'Absolutely, it's as if she needs to get this out of her system before she can move on.'

Nathaniel drove in silence for a time; both of them immersed in their own thoughts. Louise realised how painful all this must be for Nathaniel, but he was obviously still prepared to do what he could to help Marilena.

The Dakars were amazing too. They had been through so much, but they still put Marilena first, at a time when they ought to have been thinking about retirement. It must be so incredibly hard for them both.

Louise must have dozed off, because the next thing she knew they were pulling up outside Grace's house.

'It's got to be an early night for you!' Nathaniel teased.

She climbed out and went to collect her case from the boot of his car. She had flung her open bag in there too, and some of the things had spilled out. She suddenly saw the scarf she was supposed to have given to Marilena.

Her hand flew to her mouth.

'Oh, my goodness, I've forgotten . . . '

Nathaniel followed her gaze and his expression immediately altered.

'Where did you find that' he demanded in a voice of steel.

She swallowed. 'I — I was supposed to have . . . '

'You've been snooping amongst my things, haven't you?'

'No — that is — Grace said you wouldn't mind . . . '

'Well, Grace was wrong,' he told her furiously. 'I do mind! As a matter of fact, I mind very much! You had absolutely no right to pry!'

He snatched up the scarf. 'And this — this has absolutely nothing to do with you — *do you understand?*'

Nathaniel was practically shaking with anger and Louise just stood there, as if rooted to the spot, watching him helplessly. She did not know how to handle the situation. She desperately wanted to take his hand and tell him she was sorry, but didn't dare in case it made matters even worse.

'Louise your sister's on the phone — I've told her to hang on for a minute,' Grace called from the front door.

Louise grabbed her case and bag and thankfully hurried towards the house. Her last glimpse of Nathaniel was of him standing pressing the scarf to his cheek, a stern, faraway expression in his eyes. She knew that her explanations would have been wasted on him at that moment, and tears blurred her eyes. It had been a lovely weekend. She had felt she was getting to know Nathaniel but now it had been ruined.

11

'For someone who's just had the weekend off, you don't look too happy. Didn't it go as planned?' Ryan asked encountering Louise on the stairs.

'Hi Ryan — I'm just tired, that's all,' she told him irritably. This was true because she'd had another restless night going over the events of the previous evening.

'I see, well I was going to ask you if you wanted to go for a drive tonight and then have a drink in an awesome little pub I know down by the river.'

'Not tonight, some other time, Ryan. There are things I'll have to do this evening, but thanks all the same.'

'Hmm, someone's rattled your cage. Are you sure you don't want to tell me all about it?'

'No, it's fine. Thanks for the invitation, but I really do need some catchup time at home. Now, if you don't mind, I must get back to the upstairs gallery, because Arlene's not in the best of moods this morning either.'

Ryan whistled. 'I'd better keep out of the way of the pair of you then!'

Louise hadn't meant to be so grouchy, but she'd dozed fitfully the previous night and woken up with a headache. Arlene had her running about all morning.

At lunchtime, Louise purchased some sandwiches and a takeaway coffee in the cafeteria and went to sit in the gardens opposite the museum to clear her head.

She was at a loss as to how to put matters right with Nathaniel. Surely he hadn't seriously thought she'd taken the scarf for herself? Of course, with hindsight, Louise realised it would have been better if Mary had had a word with him first, before asking her to give the scarf to Marilena.

Anyway, perhaps it was for the best that she had forgotten to give it to the girl, because it might have led to a whole barrage of awkward questions that she would have felt unable to answer.

Louise sighed. Now she was going to have to speak to Mary Dakar and explain the whole unfortunate incident to her. What a mess!

As if that wasn't bad enough, Louise's sister, Joanne, had sensed there was something wrong the previous evening, when she'd phoned, and had jumped to conclusions.

'Grace said you'd been out all weekend with a friend. I tried getting you on your mobile, but it was switched off. You've got a new man in your life, haven't you, Lou?'

And when there was silence from Louise, Joanne had said triumphantly 'I knew it! Louise! It's only been a short while since you were involved with that creep, Ashley, and now you're seeing someone else and suffering heartache all over again. Don't deny it! I can tell from your voice that you're upset. Mum and Dad are so worried about you. All they want is for you to settle down and be happy.'

'Not everyone can be like you and marry the first man they date,' Louise had pointed out, fighting back the tears. Joanne had known Chris at school and they were both well suited. By the time they were eighteen they were engaged, and married when they were twenty.

'Just don't expect us to pick up the pieces when it all goes wrong,' implored Joanne, and after a brief rejoinder, Louise had replaced the receiver.

Grace had seen the mutinous expression on Louise's face and wisely refrained from making any comment — except to enquire if she wanted any supper.

Louise sighed heavily and dropping her sandwich wrapper and coffee cup in the litter bin, returned to the museum.

'Ah, there you are,' Arlene greeted her.

'Am I late?' Louise asked, consulting her watch, which always seemed to differ from the clock in the gallery.

'No — I just hadn't realised you'd gone out, and I need to speak with you urgently.'

Louise's heart sank, as she tried to think of what she might have done to annoy Arlene now, but to her amazement, her senior smiled.

'Actually, Louise, I was going to ask if you could do me a small favour.'

Louise was taken aback. She couldn't imagine how she could do Arlene Miles a favour. 'Well, naturally I will, if I can.'

'Hang on — you don't know what it is yet,' Arlene said abruptly. 'I applied to go on a course, months back, but it was very popular and I didn't get a place — anyway, someone's dropped out and, as I was on the waiting list, I've been asked if I'm still interested. I realise it's short notice — being this Wednesday and next, but, I was wondering if you could help me out?'

Louise frowned. 'But, I'm already working this Wednesday,' she pointed out.

Arlene nodded. 'Yes, I do realise that — I've checked the rotas, but you're off next Wednesday, aren't you? Actually,' she continued as Louise nodded, 'it's not that straightforward. I'd arranged to attend the preview of our new exhibition that's on downstairs. It's taking place this Wednesday evening and the Friends of Whitchurch Museum have been invited.'

Light dawned. 'So you'd like me to take your place? Well, I'm sure I can do that . . . ' She trailed off as she saw the expression on Arlene's face. 'I mean, of course, I'll stand in for you and do my best . . . ' she floundered.

Arlene hesitated. 'Actually, there is just one more thing — I've asked Nathaniel Prentice to my place for lunch, Sunday week, but now I've discovered I'm on duty here in the afternoon. I realise you might have made other plans but if not . . . '

Louise swallowed. She hadn't failed to notice the gleam in Arlene's eyes as she imparted this piece of information. 'But I don't understand, we're closed on Sundays,' she said, trying desperately not to react to the news that Arlene would be cooking lunch for Nathaniel.

'Usually, yes, but this is a group of historians who are from Derbyshire. Dr Dakar fixed it up months ago. It's friend of his who's leading the group. They just want a tour, en route to Dover. Ryan will be here too and a couple of the canteen staff have volunteered to provide refreshments. Perhaps I could do your Saturday this week to compensate?'

'I was under the impression that you thought I'd had more than my fair share of Saturdays, Arlene,' Louise remarked.

The older woman looked slightly uncomfortable. 'I suppose that, on this occasion, we could make an exception to the rule. Anyway, it's entirely up to you, of course, but I really do need an answer now.

Louise felt bone-weary. She suddenly couldn't have cared less which days she worked. She just wished she could escape off on a course like Arlene, and that it would be on Thursdays so that she wouldn't have to face Nathaniel.

The problem was she was becoming increasingly attracted to him. Perhaps it was on the rebound from Ashley. It certainly wasn't leading anywhere and, after yesterday, she doubted if Nathaniel would want anything more to do with her. Even if it wasn't strictly her fault; he'd obviously made up his mind that it was. It was obvious he was far more interested in Arlene.

She realised that Arlene was giving her a curious look and took a grip of herself. 'Sorry Arlene. I'm just a bit jaded — busy weekend. Yes that'll be fine — just let me know what I've got to do.'

* ★ *

By the time Louise got home that evening she was nearly asleep on her feet. She promised herself a really early night. Grace had gone out; leaving her supper in the oven. She ate her meal, barely tasting it, and had just made herself a cup of coffee when the doorbell rang. Mary Dakar stood on the step.

'I hope you don't mind, dear, but I've been wondering how you'd got on at the weekend. Philip's champing at the bit for news, so I've left a friend with him and here I am. Actually, I had a rather strange telephone conversation with Nathaniel.'

'Yes, I think I can guess what *that* was about,' Louise said wearily. 'I was hoping to have an opportunity to talk to you about it.'

She showed Mary into the sitting room and went to make more coffee.

'I take it Nathaniel mentioned the scarf?' Louise said handing Mary her drink a few minutes later.

Mary nodded. 'It's my fault. I take full responsibility. I should have realised Nat would want to give it to Marilena himself, along with the photograph album.'

'He seems to think I was prying, but I wouldn't do that. I didn't realise he would mind quite so much. It's a shame because, apart from that we had a good weekend.'

Mary helped herself to a biscuit. 'I take it you just forgot to give the scarf to Marilena?'

'Yes, it must have fallen out of my bag into the boot of Nathaniel's car. I've got this horrible feeling he thinks I was going to keep it for myself.'

'Well, you'd hardly have taken it with you to flaunt it at him, would you now?'

'No, of course not. It was just a silly misunderstanding,' Louise said miserably.

'And he realises that now. It's a pity, because I thought the two of you were beginning to get on well.'

'We are — we were,' Louise said so sadly that Mary reached out and patted her hand.

'Things have a habit of sorting themselves out, my dear . . . Now, just tell me about the weekend so that I can relate it to Philip, and then I'll leave you in peace. You look absolutely shattered.'

Louise felt considerably better about

things when she'd spoken with Mary. She had given her an edited version of events and assured her that Marilena was coping well at school, but had decided to say nothing about the girl's insistence that she was going to Crete in the holidays.

'It sounds as if things went really well with Marilena. Philip and I really appreciate you being there for her. She's obviously taken to you and it's good for her to have someone younger than me to relate to. Now, don't you worry about Nathaniel,' Mary advised. 'Even after all these years he's still a bit emotionally fragile where Fleur's concerned — presumably just as you are about your ex-partner?'

Louise smiled at her wanly, but made no further comment.

Mary touched her arm. 'Sometimes things happen for a reason, my dear. Anyway, enough of that, let's talk about something else for a few minutes. What have you been up to at work today?'

When Louise mentioned going to the

preview in Arlene's place on Wednesday night, Mary immediately invited her to supper.

'I'm a Friend of the Museum and you'd be doing me a great favour if you'd accompany me, Louise. Philip would want me to go and I know Keith, our next door neighbour, will keep him company so I don't have to worry about leaving him on his own.'

There was a purposeful look in Mary's eyes, but Louise was far too tired to notice. She went to bed with a lighter heart and slept like a log, awaking refreshed and much more like her old self.

★   ★   ★

The following evening she received a phone call from her mother.

'Louise, it seems such a long time since we last saw you. Your father and I are thinking of spending a few days in London soon. Is there any chance that you might have some free time — say at the beginning of next month?'

They discussed dates. 'I'm a bit tied up on Saturdays, but I could see you on the Sunday, and perhaps do a swap and get the Monday off as well.' Louise told her mother, consulting her diary.

'Actually, Grace said you'd be welcome to stay with her any time you came to visit. She's got a spare bedroom and she'd make you very welcome. She loves company.'

'Oh, I'm not sure about that. We wouldn't want to impose and it's not as if we know Grace,' her mother said doubtfully.

Louise laughed. 'Well, now's your opportunity. I know she'd like to meet you both. Anyway, have a think and let me know. You'll like her.'

They chatted for a time and Louise got the distinct feeling that her mother was getting round to telling her something.

'Mum is anything the matter?' she asked at last.

There was a silence at the end of the

line and then her mother said, 'Yes, you've guessed. Darling, don't get upset, but I think you ought to know that your father saw an announcement in the paper. It seems Ashley's got engaged to that Australian woman — Erin somebody or other — and they're obviously back in this country.'

Louise swallowed. 'Oh, I see, well, I won't be invited to the wedding so I shouldn't worry.'

'But we do, dear. He treated you so badly, breaking off your engagement like that. Mind you — as I understand it, it wasn't for the first time. I suspect he's left a string of broken hearts wherever he's been.'

'Thanks Mum, that makes me feel a whole lot better,' Louise told her wryly.

When she put down the phone, she wondered why she didn't feel more upset and realised it was because she really was getting over Ashley Harper-Jones at last. She knew that Nathaniel was ten times the person he was ever likely to be. She remembered the light touch of his lips on hers and wished it could have been for real.

★　★　★

When Louise turned up at Mary's on Wednesday for supper she saw Nathaniel's car parked outside and nearly turned tail. Louise told herself sternly that she was going to have to face him sooner or later and better now than the following afternoon when they were setting up for his lecture. She braced herself and rang the doorbell.

'How's Dr Dakar?' she enquired after she and Mary had exchanged greetings.

'I'm afraid It's going to be a long, slow road to recovery. He's had a walk this afternoon so now he's upstairs resting, but he's quite cheerful and determined to join us for supper.'

Mary showed her into the sitting room and Nathaniel looked up from *The Sun* newspaper he was reading, startled surprise written all over his face.

'Now, I've got things to attend to in

the kitchen,' Mary informed them. 'No, stay there, Louise, and talk to Nathaniel. I'm sure you've got plenty to say to each other!' And Mary hurried out of the room.

'Shades of Harriet Shawcross,' Nathaniel murmured, and winked at her.

Louise relaxed. 'About what happened on Sunday . . . ' she began.

'Forget it,' he advised. 'Seeing that scarf just brought back a few memories, and I'm afraid I jumped to all the wrong conclusions.'

Getting to his feet he caught her hands between his. 'Am I forgiven?'

'I'm not sure about that,' she told him. 'It wasn't my fault. I suppose Mary's explained to you what happened and contrived this meeting between us?'

He nodded. 'I guess she's getting a bit fed up with acting as mentor and peacemaker when she's got so many problems of her own to deal with. I'm truly sorry for letting my feelings cloud my judgement. It was all a long time ago and life has to go on.' He pressed her hand to his lips.

Her heart was hammering wildly. Releasing her hand, he reached up and touched her lips with a finger so that shock waves pulsated through her.

'It's OK, we've cleared the air and so now can we be friends?'

'I was hoping you'd say that,' Louise said, her pulse racing.

Philip came into the sitting room at that point looking frail, but obviously pleased to be back in his own surroundings. The four of them enjoyed a perfectly congenial meal, and Mary seemed visibly relieved.

Nathaniel confirmed the date of the lecture at Marilena's school and Philip Dakar told Louise how much he would appreciate it if she could take Mary's place.

Soon afterwards, Philip's neighbour arrived to spend the evening with him, and Nathaniel took Mary to the museum, whilst Louise made her own way there, so that she could drive straight home afterwards.

It was a pleasant evening, made even

more so by knowing that Nathaniel was standing beside her for much of it.

'You're getting very chummy with Nathaniel Prentice,' Ryan commented when Nathaniel had gone off with Mary to talk with some mutual acquaintances of theirs.

'Nathaniel's friendly with everyone,' Louise told him, and sipped her cranberry juice, knowing that she was going to have to take great care to keep her feelings for Nathaniel hidden.

'If you say so. Anyway, how come you're here tonight, instead of Arlene?'

She helped herself to another chicken goujon and explained about Arlene's course.

Ryan raised his eyebrows. 'I've never met anyone so keen to go on courses as Arlene Miles. Don't let her play on your good nature, Louise.'

'I don't mind,' she told him, refraining from mentioning that she'd got another Saturday free or he might feel obliged to offer to take her out again, and she just wanted a bit of space. She felt bad for thinking that way. After all, she'd enjoyed the evening she spent with Ryan and he'd been kind enough to pay for the meal. Perhaps she was being a bit harsh on him.

Soon after that the evening broke up and Nathaniel came across to say goodbye, telling Louise he'd see her the following afternoon.

* * *

The next morning, Louise spent a few boring hours disassembling one of the exhibitions in the upstairs gallery, in readiness for a new one. Arlene found fault with everything she did and ended up by saying tartly, 'Well, let's hope you manage to get your act together by this evening. We don't want a repeat of last time's debacle, do we now?'

Louise bit back a sharp retort and, as soon as she could, escaped to the lecture room. Nathaniel had warned her that he might be a bit late that afternoon, so she reorganised the room according to the plan he'd left her and, after doing the photocopying, checked it carefully before locking it away in one of the cupboards.

The evening got off to a flying start. Nathaniel had the knack of making everything so incredibly interesting. He talked about the most up-to-date finds in Kent, including a seventh century cemetery, which had been discovered during archaeological investigations at the Ebbsfleet Channel Tunnel Rail Link.

It was practically the coffee break when the door opened and a man slipped into the room and propped himself against the wall. Louise was shocked when she saw who it was. She paled and sank onto a nearby seat. Everyone was studying the worksheets for the second half of the session.

Looking in Louise's direction, Nathaniel saw that she had gone chalk white and seemed to have shrunk back into the chair.

'Louise, what's wrong? Don't you feel well?' he whispered in concern.

'That man who's just come in — I can't imagine how he's managed to track me down!' She whispered when she'd found her voice.

Nathaniel glanced across the room and stiffened as he caught sight of the small, broad-shoulder man with cropped blonde hair, lounging against the wall. Surely it couldn't be?

'I don't believe it. That's Ashley Harper-Jones . . . Do you know him, Louise?' he asked incredulously.

'Oh, yes, I know him all right,' she said between gritted teeth. 'He's the man who ruined my life!'

For a moment Nathaniel did not reply, unable to process what he was hearing, but then he said, 'Not just yours, Louise. I'm sure he didn't come here to find you. It's Philip Dakar he's after! Sit right there.'

Usually, some of the keenest members of the audience waylaid Nathaniel during the coffee break, but on this occasion he said, 'Now, Ladies and Gentlemen, there'll be plenty of time for questions shortly. If you'll excuse me, there's something I need to attend to before we begin the second half . . . '

He turned to Louise. 'Just stay by me,' he said softly, 'I promise it'll be all right.'

Louise trusted Nathaniel implicitly, but had no idea what was going on. She got to her feet, her legs like jelly.

Everyone dispersed to the coffee shop except for Louise, Nathaniel and Ashley Harper-Jones who walked purposefully across the room towards them, pale blue eyes glinting.

'Well, hello Lulu. So this is where you've been hiding! You're the last person I expected to see here tonight. You've obviously fallen on your feet!'

12

Louise couldn't reply, even if she'd chosen to do so, because it felt as if her tongue was glued to the roof of her mouth.

Ashley laughed rather nastily at her discomfiture and Louise wondered what on earth she'd ever seen in him.

'You needn't worry; it isn't you I've come here to see — although it's always pleasant to bump into old conquests. No, my business is with Philip Dakar. Where is he?'

'Dr Dakar is ill. You can tell me what it is you want,' Nathaniel said authoritatively.

Ashley looked him up and down. 'Ah, of course — it's Prentice, isn't it? Dakar's right hand man! You can give him a message from me. I'm getting married soon and a valuable heirloom — that belonged to my grandmother

— was never returned to my family's possession. I've tried asking Philip Dakar as has our solicitor, but he seems to be having a problem with his memory. Now, I'm going to ask you if you might just happen to know where it is.'

'I'm afraid you've had a wasted journey,' Nathaniel told him coolly. 'I haven't got the remotest idea of what you're talking about.'

'If you say so. You might change your tune when you realise I mean business.'

'Look this is neither the time nor the place,' Nathaniel told him. 'I'll pass your message on to the Dakars, but I'm sure if they had any property belonging to your family it would have been returned long ago. Now, if you wouldn't mind, I'm in the middle of a lecture.'

Ashley's lip curled. 'Hmm — and I wonder what your audience would think if I told them what I know about you?'

Louise saw Nathaniel clench his fists, and how his lips were tightly closed. The grandfather clock in the corner ticked loudly, filling in the silence. She took a deep breath and said:

'Ashley, if I were you, I'd return to the hole you crawled out from. It's obvious you're not going to get anywhere by hanging around here. Oh, and congratulations on your latest engagement, by the way. I really hope Erin knows what she's getting herself in for.' And, without a backward glance, she strode from the room with all the dignity she could muster, signalling to the steward hovering just outside the door.

'Show that man off the premises, would you Nigel? He's being a nuisance and isn't allowed here due to a past incident.'

Nigel nodded. 'It'd be a pleasure. I encountered him once many years ago — never forget a face. He's a troublemaker of the first degree. That's why I've been hanging about. If he refuses to leave quietly, I'll call the police . . . Just as Mr Prentice is finding his feet back in Whitchurch again, too.'

Nigel who had worked at the museum

for many years remembered the incident only too well and immediately sprang into action. He was a very large, powerfully built man. Louise couldn't hear what was said, but a disgruntled Ashley Harper-Jones left shortly afterwards, muttering obscene threats.

'My goodness, Louise, you were right on cue,' Nathaniel said, as he caught up with her.

'Well, I could see that you wanted to thump him and that wouldn't have achieved anything, would it? Apart from adding a bit of additional spice to your lecture . . . Actually, I'm feeling a bit shaky.'

Nathaniel steered her to the nearest seat and she sank onto it thankfully. He went off and returned shortly afterwards with a couple of coffees, warding off a member of the public who was bursting to ask him a question.

'Louise, we need to talk urgently, but it's going to have to wait. I'll try to finish sharply tonight — think up some excuse. Perhaps we can go for a drink.

There are things I'm burning to ask.'

'Yes, I can imagine.' She sighed and gratefully sipped her coffee. 'There are quite a few things I need to ask you, too. It seems we might have even more in common than we thought!'

He gave a little laugh. 'If by that you mean we're both the victims of circumstances beyond our control — to say nothing of a bizarre coincidence, then apparently so.'

How they got through the remainder of the evening, Louise would never know. She tried desperately hard to concentrate on the rest of Nathaniel's talk and to join in, as they looked at the human history collections in the museum, but her head was spinning. Dr Dakar had known all along about the connection between herself and Ashley Harper-Jones, but now it seemed that Ashley was the man who had been engaged to Fleur as well.

Eventually, the evening drew to a close. Louise admired Nathaniel for the way he had conducted the second half, as if nothing had happened, but she had seen the way that Ashley's visit had affected him, and realised that it was taking every ounce of his self-control to carry on as normal.

They packed away in record time with the help of the stewards who had attended the lecture. Nathaniel thanked Nigel again for ejecting Ashley from the building so efficiently.

Arlene came over to congratulate Nathaniel on the evening and then turned to Louise. 'Was there a problem earlier on with that latecomer?'

'No, he had just wandered in off the street without a ticket and was making a bit of a nuisance of himself. Nigel dealt with him,' Nathaniel assured her.

Arlene frowned and looked from one to the other. 'I see — right, I'll say goodnight then.'

Louise waited until she'd gone and raced off to the bathroom where she splashed her hot face with water, did some running repairs to her make-up and grabbing her jacket, went to wait in the entrance hall. Shortly afterwards, Nathaniel appeared, and she walked with him to the car park.

'I thought a café would be better than a pub which could be a bit noisy at this time of night. If you like, you can leave your car here and I'll drive you home. Can you take a bus in the morning?'

She nodded. It seemed that Nathaniel knew of an all-night café where they could get coffee and toasted sandwiches. It was a pleasant, clean place with pine panelling on the walls, red and white checked tablecloths and quiet music. They placed their order and sat in a quiet corner with their coffees.

'Do you want to go first or shall I?' Nathaniel asked after a few moments silence.

Louise swallowed a mouthful of coffee, her stomach churning. 'Ok, I'll go first. I'll try to answer whatever questions you ask. I'm only surprised the Dakars haven't told you about me already.'

'The Dakars are the very souls of discretion. They just told me you'd had a rough time concerning your previous place of work. I realise now that Ashley Harper-Jones was involved. Would you care to elaborate?'

Louise nodded and took a deep breath. 'As you've no doubt realised from our conversation this evening, Ashley and I were in a relationship — engaged to be married. I suppose I was very naïve. I'm afraid he swept me off my feet, and I was so gullible that I believed every word he told me.'

She filled Nathaniel in as briefly as possible, speaking in such a low tone that he had to lean across the table to catch what she said.

'I was working in Yorkshire at the home of the Harper-Jones family. It's a beautiful place — a minor stately home, and I enjoyed my work there which involved setting up exhibitions, and being a tour guide. After I'd been there for about eighteen months, Ashley turned up out of the blue. Apparently, he'd been in Australia. Anyway, as I've already said, he completely swept me off my feet — persuaded his father to finance him in a project; the London Art Gallery, and asked me to go along as the Exhibitions Manager.'

'And that's where you were before you came to Whitchurch?' Nathaniel asked, looking at her intently.

Louise nodded. 'Yeah, with hindsight, I realise I should have known better, but I imagined myself to be in love with him and was wearing rose-tinted glasses! I'd been warned about Ashley. One or two of the staff in Yorkshire knew him from when he lived there, and told me he had a reputation as womaniser, but didn't say anything more specific.'

She sighed. 'I suppose I was a bit headstrong — and chose to ignore everyone including my family. I helped set up the art gallery, and business was fairly brisk for a time. It didn't matter to me that Ashley was only paying me a low salary, because he said he needed to plough as much as he could back into the business, but, after a while, I did wonder about his extravagant lifestyle.

'To be fair, I had a wonderful time; he took me to places I'd never been to before, and I mixed with people I'd never have met in the normal run of circumstances. It wasn't long before he proposed and we were planning our wedding and future together. I'd never been so happy.'

'And then?' Nathaniel prompted gently.

'We'd been together for almost a year when things began to change. One day, a very glamorous, red-haired Australian woman came into the gallery asking for Ashley. I'll never forget the look on his face when he saw her. He seemed completely stunned.'

Louise paused to drink some of her cooling coffee and Nathaniel ordered refills from the waitress who brought their toasted sandwiches.

'It was soon after this that I realised Ashley wasn't organising any new exhibitions, and didn't seem to be selling much of the existing work on display. Then he began to stay away for longer and longer spells without telling me where he was going.

'However, he was around on the day that Philip Dakar called. I heard raised voices, and Philip came storming out of Ashley's office looking absolutely furious. That was when he gave me his card and told me to contact him if ever I decided to move on. At the time I didn't think too much of it, but now it all makes perfect sense.

'So what happened next?' Nathaniel prompted.

'Ashley told me not to worry about Dr Dakar — just a silly argument about nothing, he said. Anyway things seemed to go on a downward spiral after that and then there was that dreadful day when Ashley told me he was giving up the gallery because the business was failing and he was in danger of losing all his father's money. He even asked me for a loan, but I didn't have any capital to speak of. And then he dropped the bombshell — told me that it was all over between us. He'd made a big mistake. Now that he'd met Erin — the Australian woman again, he realised it was her he wanted to be with and not me.'

Louise's voice broke and she struggled for control. She buried her head in her hands and Nathaniel waited for her to compose herself.

'So you see what a fool I've been, but I really thought Ashley was genuine. After all, he'd asked me to marry him. I felt such an utter fool. I had no home, no job and didn't know what to do other than to go back to live with my parents. I didn't want that, after being independent, so that's when I contacted Dr Dakar.'

Nathaniel settled back in his chair, hands behind his head. 'That's unbelievable! It's almost a repeat performance of what happened to Fleur. I wonder how many others there have been in between!'

Louise stared at him, eyes bright with unshed tears. 'So, I was right — that is what you meant. Is — is Ashley Harper-Jones, Marilena's father?'

Nathaniel shrugged. 'We'll never know for sure without a paternity test, and he's not likely to agree to that but, as far as we can establish, yes. Fleur was not promiscuous — of that I'm certain.'

Louise was stunned and sat for a moment staring into space. 'And Dr Dakar has done all this for me — after everything he and Mary have been through?'

'Philip is a very caring person. Ashley seems to leave destruction in his wake and to have no conscience. He mentioned he wants to reclaim a precious heirloom — presumably the necklace, but what could be more precious than Marilena?'

'Absolutely! I realised belatedly, that he obviously values material possessions more than what's really important in life!' she exclaimed angrily. 'Well, I'm glad to be rid of him!'

'Good for you!' There was sympathy in Nathaniel's rich brown eyes. 'I wondered what it was that had made you look so sad when we first met. Now I know. Let's hope he treats the new woman in his life with more consideration and compassion,' he added sombrely.

'I knew he didn't want children, but I thought I could work on him,' Louise murmured. 'Anyway, that's all in the past, and I suspect Marilena's better off not knowing him. That woman he's just got engaged to, Erin, is the same one he was involved with in Australia — before he met me. She was the reason for us splitting up. She came all the way to London to find him again.'

'Then let's hope that for her sake he actually sticks with her this time. Now, Louise, I know this has come as a shock to you, as indeed it has to me, but will it make any difference to our friendship?'

She picked up a toasted sandwich suddenly feeling ridiculously hungry.

'Of course not — why ever should it?'

He paused. 'Because — surely, you must have heard the speculation about Fleur and me?'

She met the gaze of his dark brown

eyes, 'Let's not even go there, Nathaniel. I know that the Dakars wouldn't even give you house room if they believed you hadn't been honest with them. They've entrusted you with Marilena and, to prove it, they've made you her godfather.'

He reached across the table and took her hands between his. 'Thank you, Louise. That means a lot to me. It's taken me a long time to shake off the past and to move on, but I've managed to do so. I can assure you that those rumours have no substance. There have been other women in my life since, but no-one to match up with Fleur until now.'

Louise looked at him, what could he mean — dared she hope he was referring to her?

'Whatever else Ashley Harper-Jones may not have been there's one thing in his favour. He's very good at selecting lovely women who have proved to be far too good for him.'

Louise lowered her eyes, afraid of what she might see if she met Nathaniel's dark brown eyes. In that moment she felt a surge of emotion engulf her and realised it wasn't just because of Ashley turning up at the museum like that; it was mostly because Nathaniel was sitting across the table from her, stroking the back of her hand and making her feel more feminine and wanted than she had done for months. Something still puzzled her.

'This — this heirloom that Ashley is trying to locate. Why does he think Philip Dakar has got it, when he's stated so clearly that he hasn't?'

'I'm not sure,' Nathaniel said at last. It's something I'm going to have to mention to Mary first of all. We can't risk upsetting Philip when he's been so very ill. The problem is — Ashley Harper-Jones sounded as if he meant business, and that he doesn't intend to take no for an answer. Perhaps he has new information as to the whereabouts of that necklace. It's probably something to do with the wedding,' Nathaniel picked up the bill. 'Anyway, I think we've said enough for one evening, don't you? Are you ready to go home now?'

Louise nodded. 'Yes, please. It's been quite an evening.'

As they drove the short distance to Grace's house he said, 'When we were at Mary's on Wednesday evening, I gathered that you're free again on Saturday. I've had a thought about that — I realise it's very short notice, how about I take you for that promised trip to see the Brighton Pavilion? It might help to take your mind off things.'

'Yes, please — I'd like that very much, Nathaniel, but don't feel you've got to,' she said unsteadily.

Louise hoped she didn't sound too enthusiastic, as her heart thumped wildly.

The amber lights in his eyes glinted. 'I rarely do anything unless I want to,' he told her lightly. 'I'd be glad of your company. 'Good — that's settled then and are you still up to accompany me to the lecture at Marilena's school?'

'Absolutely. I'm looking forward to it.'

Louise felt a warm glow of happiness inside her until she remembered that he was having lunch with Arlene Miles the following Sunday. So just make the most of it, she told herself.

As Louise zipped up her jacket she asked, 'What happens if Ashley turns up again? I truly don't want to see him and it could make things awkward for me at work.'

'I think Ashley was equally as surprised to see you, as you were to see him this evening. Hopefully, he's got the message now and will stay away from the museum. He doesn't have the Dakar's address or phone number. They've moved since Marilena was born — so we'll just have to hope he stays away.'

* * *

Louise was signing in at the museum the following morning when Arlene appeared in the reception area, just as Ryan walked through the door.

'There you are, Louise,' Arlene

greeted her. 'I've been looking for you everywhere. I saw your car when I arrived just after eight, so assumed you must be already in the building.'

'Don't assume anything, Arlene,' Ryan told her, taking the pen from Louise and signing his name with a flourish. 'For all you know, Louise might have stayed at my place last night!'

Louise wanted to chuckle when she saw the expression on Arlene's face, but then she realised her senior would probably take him seriously and wished Ryan hadn't been so flippant.

'Right, I'm here now so what would you like me to do?' she asked Arlene sternly.

It seemed that Louise was to act as steward in the costume gallery, because Polly, who usually worked there, was off on a course. Louise didn't mind this at all. She had acquainted herself with it on several occasions, because it was a firm favourite with parties of school children, and she knew it was earmarked for alterations whenever the funds became available. Arlene, however, wasn't at all pleased at having to spare her for the entire morning, as they were in the middle of creating a new display in one of the upstairs galleries, and now the workload would fall on her.

To Louise's surprise, at around eleven o'clock, just as she was thinking about taking a coffee break, Nathaniel came into the costume gallery. She felt her heart leap at the sight of him.

'Hi again. How are you this morning, Louise? I thought you'd be upstairs, but when I went there just now, Arlene told me you'd been instructed to work down here this morning.

Louise nodded and wondered what had brought him to the museum that morning. He came to look over her shoulder and she was so aware of his presence that she hardly dared breathe.

'Those displays are looking decidedly weary. I suppose there just isn't enough funding to update them.'

'Not for the present, no, although it has been noted. Maintaining the main exhibition areas takes priority, but, personally, I think this is in serious need of an urgent makeover,' Louise told him. 'Goodness knows when it last had a refit. It's an extremely popular area.'

'Hmm!' He stood there, hands in pockets, a thoughtful expression on his face. I've been to see the Dakars just now. Philip's doing remarkably well now he's back home. I managed to talk with Mary on her own for a few minutes about yesterday's visitor.'

'And?' Louise prompted impatiently.

Fortunately, the area was empty apart from them. 'There's been nothing new. Obviously, she was as shocked as we were to learn that Harper-Jones had turned up at the museum last night. She just reiterated what we already know — that one of the last things Fleur said to Philip before she died, was that there was something of value in her bag that she wanted him to keep safe for Marilena. They only ever found a letter from Ashley's grandmother, stating that she'd given the necklace to

Fleur. It's a mystery as to what became of it.'

'Mary mentioned the letter to me,' Louise said. 'How sad that the grandmother died. She seemed very supportive of Fleur.'

Nathaniel nodded. 'As you can imagine, when Fleur died, the Dakars were too distraught to even think about the necklace. The Harper-Jones family haven't been at all cooperative and everything's been dealt with via their solicitor.

'Ashley was quick to deny that he was Marilena's father. If only Elinor Harper-Jones — his grandmother — had still been alive things might have been very different, but she'd had a stroke shortly after returning to England and died shortly after Marilena was born.'

'It just seems odd that Ashley is still pursuing this business of the missing necklace after all this time.'

Nathaniel nodded. 'I agree. Of course, the original letter is with the Dakar's solicitor, but, unfortunately for them; when he was sorting out Fleur's affairs he felt legally obliged to send a copy to the Harper-Jones family, with its reference to the missing necklace. And, from then on, the Harper-Jones solicitor began to contact the Dakar's solicitor, requesting that it be found and returned, as it was indeed a valuable heirloom and part of the family collection of jewels.'

'But surely if the letter verifies that it was given to Fleur when Elinor Harper-Jones was still alive, then that carried some weight?'

Nathaniel shook his head. 'Mary told me something this morning that I wasn't aware of. It seems that the grandmother's letter to Fleur would not stand up in a court of law because of the specific instructions regarding the family jewellery. The necklace is part of a collection and it has to remain within the family.

'I agree it all seems dreadfully unjust, but the law *is* the law. Apparently, Philip and Mary have been trying to shut their mind to it — still hoping that they can claim the necklace for

Marilena as her inheritance — if it ever turns up.

'Anyway, as I said last night, Ashley doesn't know where the Dakars live. They moved shortly after Marilena was born, when they were convinced Ashley wanted nothing to do with the child — knowing that he could always contact them through their solicitor if he had a sudden change of heart.'

'I don't suppose it would be that difficult to track them down if he's a mind to,' Louise said worriedly.

'Oh, hopefully, he'll know better than to harass them after the other evening,' Nathaniel assured her and Louise could only hope he was right.

Just then, Louise was called away by one of the other stewards. She returned to find Nathaniel standing in front of one of the display cases, a curious expression on his face. He was deep in thought and didn't immediately realise she was there.

She followed his gaze to see if she could work out what had caught his attention, and saw that he was studying the Victorian and Edwardian models clad in evening wear and wedding dresses. But then she noticed the lovely necklaces about their throats . . .

13

Louise looked questioningly at Nathaniel, as he turned towards her, but just then, another group of people came into the gallery — this time pensioners on a day trip from Sussex. She did her best to answer their questions and gave them the handouts from the pocket at the side of the display case. She also pointed out the recorded information activated at the touch of a button, and then Nathaniel took her for a well-deserved cup of coffee.

★　★　★

The cafeteria was packed. 'My turn,' Louise insisted and, after what seemed like an eternity, returned with the coffee and a couple of slices of ginger cake.

'So, how come you're around today — not that I'm not pleased to see you,' she floundered.

He laughed at her discomfiture. 'I'm having a day off. Decided to get some preparation done for my lecture next Thursday, so that I'm free to enjoy the weekend. You still keen to go out tomorrow?'

'Absolutely. I'm looking forward to it.'

'Only I wouldn't like to keep you away from Ryan.' He gave her an odd look. 'Actually, I'm a bit mystified, Louise, because Arlene is under the impression that you went home with him last night; whereas I distinctly remember dropping you off at Grace's.'

'Arlene really is the limit!' Louise exclaimed crossly. 'She needs to learn to mind her own business!'

'That's not very charitable, Louise,' he reproved. 'Apparently, Ryan hinted as much.'

'Oh, he was just winding her up. She saw my car outside before I arrived this morning and wondered where I was, that's all. Not that it's anybody's concern.'

'No,' he said meekly, 'you're quite right.' He finished his coffee. 'Thanks for the refreshments. I'll pick you up tomorrow around eight o'clock unless you've changed your mind about our trip to Brighton. If you still want to come, I can make sure you're back here late afternoon — if you've a date with Ryan in the evening.'

She raised her eyebrows. 'I thought you were going to mind your own business!' She said rudely, and he laughed.

'I've inherited my natural curiosity from my mother! Not my fault if it's in my genes!' He got to his feet. 'Actually, I wouldn't mind taking another look at the costume gallery before I get on with what I came here to do.'

When they reached the costume gallery, Nathaniel stood in front of the cases again; peering at the models for such a long time that Louise could not imagine what he was looking at. After answering a couple of queries from a middle-aged couple, she crossed to his side.

'What in particular interests you?' she asked, puzzled.

The couple hadn't lingered and, for the moment, they had the gallery to themselves.

'Supposing someone wanted to hide something in a hurry . . . '

She followed his train of thought. 'You mean Fleur Dakar? But surely, if the necklace had been hidden here, after all these years, it would have been discovered. Anyway, Dr Dakar must surely have had the same idea as you.'

'I would have assumed so, but just supposing he hasn't? Are these cases alarmed?'

'I'm not sure — you'd need to ask Nigel or one of the other stewards. The costumes are probably worth a few hundred pounds, but the jewellery is just paste and glass — at least . . . '

Nathaniel shot her a look. 'Are you quite sure about that? I'm no expert on jewellery, but I could take a look. I think I can tell the genuine article when I see it. Do you happen to know if there's any more — apart from what's displayed in here?'

'Only the very ancient stuff and you already know about that. Most of that's only replica too, because, as I'm sure you're aware, the authentic items are in the British Museum.'

Nathaniel rubbed his chin. 'Of course it would help if we knew exactly what we were looking for. *Some sort of necklace*, is a little vague. Mary Dakar told me that Fleur was brought to the museum by someone — probably a homeless person. It seems she'd been living rough.'

'And so she might have been robbed way before she arrived here?'

Nathaniel nodded. 'I suppose it's a possibility, but on the other hand, what if Fleur asked this friend to hide the necklace? It seems the woman disappeared before anyone could question her.'

Louise stared at him. 'Or what if Ashley removed it when they were in Crete and Fleur was trying to tell her father that. The trouble is I'm no longer sure of what he's capable of doing. Perhaps I didn't really know him at all.'

Nathaniel put an arm about her shoulders, sending a little shiver dancing along her spine. 'You've had a wretched time and it's not fair that you should be burdened with all this,' he said gently.

'I suppose Ashley and his family thought it was worth one final attempt to try to track the necklace down. Personally, I just can't believe he'd got the nerve to show his face here again.'

Nathaniel nodded. 'He must be extremely thick-skinned.'

'I can't help wondering if the argument between Ashley and Philip Dakar in London had something to do with the necklace. Maybe Ashley had been pestering the Dakar's solicitor again.'

'Perhaps, but Philip told me he'd seen Ashley's website for the art gallery on the internet so I suspect he was trying, yet again, to get Ashley to face up to his responsibilities.

Louise was staring at the jewellery adorning the models in the show cases. The replicas were very realistic. 'So supposing the real necklace is here under our very noses all the time!'

'That's what I was thinking, but, I'm afraid it's highly improbable, after thirteen years. I suppose I could always take a closer look. As I've said I don't profess to be an expert, but in my line of business at least I can tell the difference between glass and the real thing. Of course, I could always ask Julian Byrne for his expert opinion.'

'Julian Byrne?' Louise asked, mystified.

Nathaniel smiled. 'The jewellery expert we call upon from time to time. 'Obviously, we'd need to run it past Stuart Tomlinson first.'

Louise frowned in concentration. 'But what possible reason could you give to this Julian? I mean those pieces must have been catalogued'

'Oh, I'll think of something that sounds plausible,' he assured her. 'Tell you what, how would it be if I have a word with Stuart now to see if I can take a look first?'

Stuart Tomlinson came into the gallery a few moments later, just as if they had conjured him up out of thin air.

'So here you are, Nat. You're a difficult man to track down.'

'Not if you know where to look,' Nathaniel jested. 'Actually, I was wondering if I could take a closer look at this jewellery. There's a bit of a question mark over the authenticity of one or two of the pieces.'

Stuart Tomlinson looked taken aback. 'I inherited this lot when I came here and I can assure you it's fake — just coloured glass, Nathaniel, but if you want to take a closer look then by all means do so.'

'It would satisfy my curiosity,' Nathaniel told him. 'So have I got your permission to remove it for an hour or so — just in case there's something that's been overlooked?'

Stuart gave a wry smile. 'By all means, but I'm certain you won't find anything of significance,' he said confidently. 'It had all been carefully catalogued when I first came here. Nothing new has been added to the collection, since, although I have to say it's high time this gallery was updated — Polly's mentioned it often enough.

'Anyway, the jewellery could do with a bit of an overhaul. I'm sure Louise will gather it all up for you — the cases aren't alarmed. We don't even have any CCTV in this area. Unbelievable — but that just proves there's nothing worth stealing. Make a note of exactly where you've taken the items from, Louise, so that they can be returned to the correct models. Oh, and you'd better put a notice on the case to say they've been removed for cleaning, before there are a stream of questions — thanks Louise.'

He took his mobile from his pocket. 'I'll just give Nigel a ring — get him to bring the keys and give you a hand.'

When he'd finished the call he turned

to Nathaniel. 'Actually, Nat, I could do with a word with you — if you can spare the time. I'd almost forgotten why I'd come in here. Someone said they'd seen you heading in this direction.'

And the two men wandered out of the gallery deep in conversation.

Nigel appeared a few moments later, clutching a box and a large bunch of keys. 'Mr Tomlinson said you might need a hand. This gallery could do with a bit of a spring clean. Polly's always going on about the state of it. How on earth did you wangle it?'

'Oh, it was Nathaniel Prentice. He seems to know how to get things done.'

'Good for him! Ok let's get this show on the road.'

'So has this display been here for a long time?' Louise enquired as Nigel struggled to open the case which was a bit stiff.

'Oh, several years at a rough guess. 'Course this gallery used to be much bigger — but then, after that little lass was born, Dr Dakar shut it off. Now no one goes beyond that screen. It's like he's keeping it as a kind of shrine to his daughter.'

Louise's head shot up. 'I'm sorry, are you telling me that Marilena Dakar was born *here* in the museum?'

Nigel looked uncomfortable. 'Sorry, if I'm speaking out of turn — thought you must know — what with you being friendly with the Dakars and Nathaniel Prentice.'

'Please don't apologise. I know most of the story. So where exactly was the baby born?'

They were interrupted by several visitors who all appeared at once and asked a seemingly endless stream of questions.

'Tell you what,' Nigel said as the party moved off. 'Why don't you come back around three thirty and I'll take you on a conducted tour — show you where we keep the rest of the stock, the clothes chests etc.'

'Love to, Nigel, but Arlene will probably need me somewhere else.'

'You should be all right there because she's going to be out around then. Going to a meeting at the Archives Centre and then off somewhere this evening — so you're perfectly safe. And I promise I won't say a word.' He touched the side of his nose.

Louise took the box of jewellery up to Philip's office where Nathaniel had said she'd find him. He gave her a winning smile and indicated the special magnifying glass on the desk.

'As you can see, I'm all prepared. I've borrowed this from Colin. Don't get your hopes up, Louise. We're probably going down the wrong path. I'll get back to you before I leave.'

Nathaniel sounded professional and detached, unlike the man she'd recently had coffee with.

Louise went back to the gallery and made a notice to fix on the display case, and then she was kept busy with several more visitors. After they'd gone, she took another look at the models. There were a fair number of cobwebs festooning the back of them so she took a feather duster and did her best, but realised the gallery would need closing, if a thorough job was to be done. The delicate costumes needed some specialist care and attention.

As she adjusted the folds of an elaborate evening gown adorning one of the Victorian ladies, she suddenly noticed the reticule around the dummy's wrist.

'Of course!' she exclaimed aloud. 'Why ever didn't I think of it before? Perhaps Fleur didn't mean the necklace was in *her* bag!'

'Sorry, Louise, did you say something?' Nigel had returned and looked up from the worksheet he was studying.

'Oh, no, it's fine . . . just talking to myself,' she said quickly.

She was itching to take a look inside the reticule but Nigel was obviously champing at the bit to get off for his lunch.

'How about you lock up now, and I'll come back here around three thirty?' she suggested. 'I might need you to open up again — if Mr Prentice has finished with the jewellery.'

'Will do! See you later then, Louise.' He grinned at her in a conspiratorial fashion and marched off.

True to his word, Nathaniel came into the gallery shortly afterwards 'I've had a quick look, Louise, but I'm afraid Stuart's right. They *are* just coloured glass — very good replicas. There's one good thing come out of this though. Stuart's decided to get them cleaned before they go back on the dummies, which means you can get off to lunch on time for once, as you won't have to replace them. Sorry to have raised your hopes, but at least it's stopped us speculating.'

Louise swallowed her disappointment. 'So — where to from here? I mean we're back to square one, aren't we?'

'I'm afraid so — anyway don't worry about it, Louise.'

Louise decided to keep her theory about the bag to herself for the time being. 'There is just one thing . . . ' She told him what Nigel had said about the back of the gallery being shut off after Marilena was born.

Nathaniel nodded. 'Yes, I had heard that's where Fleur gave birth, but the Dakars don't like to be reminded about it, so we don't mention it. You know, Louise you might just have hit on something. There must be stacks of stuff behind that screen. The space is used as a kind of storeroom nowadays for this gallery.'

'I'm coming back here this afternoon around three thirty, to take a look. Apparently, Arlene's going out so I'll need to get my jobs done before then.'

'Mmm, I can't make any promises, but if it's at all possible, I'll join you. Sorry, I've got to rush off now — people to see and things to do. Hope to be back later, but if not, I'll see you tomorrow morning bright and early.'

Shortly afterwards Arlene came into the gallery, a frown on her face. 'Are you still here, Louise? Whatever have you been doing?'

'Actually, it's been surprisingly busy here this morning. Even Mr Tomlinson came in. They're talking of revamping this gallery.'

'I wouldn't hold your breath — they've been doing that for months. Anyway, I shall need you with me for the first part of the afternoon. We're behind schedule, as it is, and our new exhibition opens next week — in case it had escaped your memory. Oh, and I'm off to a meeting at the Archives Centre at three thirty . . . Do you happen to know if Mr Prentice has gone yet? Someone said they'd seen him come in here.'

'Yes, he did pop in briefly to check on something. I'm afraid you've just missed him, Arlene,' Louise told her, and did not fail to notice the look of disappointment on Arlene's face.

'Never mind, I'll be seeing him tonight anyway,' Arlene informed her brightly and swept out of the room.

Louise stood staring after her. So Nathaniel really was involved with

Arlene. She felt a sharp pang akin to jealousy, and then she pulled herself together. After all, she still had the following day to look forward to in his company.

*   *   *

Nigel was already waiting in the costume gallery speaking to a couple of visitors when she arrived. As soon as they'd gone, he said apologetically, 'Mr Tomlinson needs me from four o'clock onwards so I'll unlock the showcases now and quickly show you the back of the gallery. Hang on whilst I close this outer door.'

There was a small padlock securing the screen at the end of the gallery. Nigel unlocked it with some difficulty. When he'd folded back the screen, Louise gasped because it was so dark inside — like a cave.

'Hang on there's a light switch around here somewhere.' Nigel located it, and as her eyes became accustomed to the gloom she could make out a quantity of dummies all dressed in costume and placed against the back wall. In front were four linen chests.

'That was the one where they laid the baby,' Nigel told her indicating the third one. 'It's kept locked now and it's quite empty except for a note giving young Marilena's date of birth. My wife was working here then, you know. Heard poor Fleur crying out and came to investigate. It was Florence that got in touch with Dr Dakar.'

Louise stared at him. 'Your wife — I hadn't realised.'

'Poor Florence found it very hard to bear when the young lass died, but there was nothing she could have done. They got her to hospital as quickly as they could.'

'I understand someone came with her to the museum,' Louise said, choosing her words carefully.

'Yes, but she scarpered when she realised what was happening . . . Sorry, Louise, but I'd best be off now. When you've done here, give me a ring on your mobile and I'll lock up and collect the keys — they're all labelled.'

Nigel was just about to leave when Nathaniel arrived. Louise didn't fancy exploring the dark area behind the screen on her own, and her heart leapt.

As soon as Nigel had gone she quickly filled Nathaniel in.

'Good thinking Louise although, after all this time, I wouldn't want you to get your hopes up. So, why don't we start here first? Just let me lock that outer door again.'

Louise climbed into the show case and looked around her. There were evening bags and reticules on a number of the models' wrists, and a further display on a raised stand in the front of the case. Systematically, they searched each one, but to their disappointment there was nothing inside except for screwed up balls of faded tissue paper and an occasional dead moth.

'Well, I think we can conclude that there's nothing here,' Nathaniel told her. 'Now let's look behind that screen.'

He battled with the lock on the first linen chest. Suddenly the clasp sprang open and he heaved up the lid to reveal clothes piled high. A musty smell pervaded the air.

'I'm afraid it's going to take us rather a long time to get through this lot,' he said, 'so I think we're going to have to leave it for another day.'

Louise nodded. She pointed out the chest where Marilena had been laid just after she was born, and told him about Nigel's wife being there.

'That's interesting, but of course, if Florence had known anything about the necklace at the time, she would have told the Dakars. She's a trusted friend.'

Louise was looking at the dummies stacked along the back wall. Something caught her attention. 'That dummy dressed as a doctor — who does he represent?'

Nathaniel followed her gaze. 'Oh, now I do know the answer to that one. That was Reginald Yates. He has a direct descendant who is still practising medicine today. Bob Yates' wife is a prominent member of the Friends of Whitchurch Museum. Mary will know the history. The problem is that, that particular dummy doesn't fit anywhere, does it? It ought to be in a different section of the museum.'

A shelf ran round the back of the gallery and on it Louise spotted a Gladstone bag. She stared at it, as a thought suddenly occurred to her.

'Nathaniel, supposing we've been barking up the wrong tree all this time!'

'How d'you mean?' he demanded. He caught her arm. 'Louise, tell me what you're thinking!'

'The Dakars found the letter about the necklace, but the solicitor maintains that without a new will it's worthless. Just supposing Marilena was given the new will as well as the necklace to bring to them . . . A will wouldn't fit into a reticule, would it now — and it wasn't in Marilena's bag.'

'But it would fit into a bag like that one!' He lifted down the bag and a cloud of dust flew into the air. 'I can't possibly see anything under this light.'

He carried it carefully into the gallery and deposited it on a narrow bench. 'Of course it would be locked!'

There were a series of small keys on the bunch Nigel had entrusted to them and, eventually, Nathaniel located one that looked as if it might fit. Louise held her breath as he eventually managed to open it.

It was full of documents relating to Dr Reginald Yates, medical practice, together with a stethoscope and a couple of small cases obviously containing instruments together with a broken thermometer.

'Wow! These ought to be in the archives upstairs. This is a find in itself. They've obviously been forgotten about, although there must be a record somewhere.'

Nathaniel carefully removed the papers and Louise began to separate them, keeping them in piles. She was on the fourth lot when a slim brown envelope was dislodged and slid to the floor.

With bated breath she picked it up. 'Nathaniel — the missing will! It's been here all the time amongst these papers in Dr Yates' bag!'

Nathaniel looked incredulous. 'Are you sure — let me see! Louise this is incredible! What an amazing find!'

'Of course without the necklace . . . '

'Let's take one step at a time. Louise, well done! Now I've got to figure out how to get this out of the museum without it being picked up on CCTV. Any ideas?'

She shook her head. 'Your jacket?'

'No — this envelope's too long and I need to keep it flat . . . hang on.'

'Nathaniel what are you doing?' she laughed as he removed his tie and handed it to her and then began to unbutton his shirt displaying a tantalising glimpse of tanned flesh.

'Where there's a *will* there's a way,' he said with a wicked smile, and stuffing it down his shirt front, rebuttoned the neck and reached for his tie; his fingers brushing hers, so that she caught her breath.

'You'll crackle,' she told him, when she could speak.

He finished knotting his tie and caught her to him. 'Let's put it to the test, shall we?'

She could feel the heat emanating from his body; her heart beat rapidly. And then he stooped and his lips met hers in a long lingering kiss that sent shock waves pulsating through her. He only released her when his mobile rang.

After a short conversation he switched it off. 'I'm supposed to be somewhere as *of now!* Louise, can you ring Nigel to lock up. I'm so sorry . . . ' His rich brown eyes met hers for a moment and held her gaze.

She wasn't sure what exactly he was apologising for, but left alone she refused to give herself time to dwell on it. She picked up a pile of documents and was about to replace them when another thought struck her and she put them down all again. Instead she upended the heavy bag carefully and tipped out the pieces of broken thermometer onto a sheet of newspaper. Then she opened the larger of the two instrument cases. Everything was neatly in its place and labelled. The smaller case was labelled *thermometer*, so why then was it loose and broken?

Her heart began to beat rapidly as she undid the clasp securing the case. With hands that trembled, she moved aside the folds of tissue paper and there, nestling inside, was an exquisite emerald and diamond necklace. She gasped. Was this what everyone was looking for? Louise stared at it in wonder. It was quite the most beautiful thing she had ever seen, but she realised that — for all she knew — it might be fake too.

She made a rapid decision and placing the necklace back in its case put it inside her handbag. Whatever would happen if someone discovered what she had done? Supposing the necklace was found on her person. How would she explain it? She tried to phone Nathaniel, but he wasn't answering either his mobile or his landline, so she left a message on his voicemail and just to make doubly certain, sent him a text as well.

Nigel came back shortly afterwards to lock up. He didn't ask any questions, but she could tell he was curious by everyone's sudden interest in the gallery.

Nathaniel still hadn't got back to her by the time she arrived at Grace's so she left him a second message — this time on his landline, but then she remembered he was seeing Arlene that evening and there was a dull ache inside her as she remembered the kiss that had briefly filled her with ecstasy. Surely it had meant something to him?

She carefully stowed the necklace in the top drawer of her bedside cabinet and spent the evening in a state of anxiety, willing for Nathaniel to ring her, but she realised he wasn't likely to do that if he was in Arlene's company.

She attempted to read but found it difficult to concentrate and the words danced before her eyes. In the end she decided to have an early night.

14

The following morning, Louise tried to appear composed, but she could barely wait for Nathaniel to arrive so that she could tell him about her second discovery. She dressed carefully in a white top and a blue denim skirt. She caught her hair back in a buckle, and then sat anxiously waiting for Nathaniel. He was ten minutes late.

'Sorry, the traffic coming through town was horrendous. Everyone must be going shopping!'

It wasn't until they were well on their way that she told him about her find.

'Louise, you do choose your moments,' he told her, skilfully overtaking a lorry.

'That's a bit unfair. 'I left a couple of messages on your answerphone and sent you a text, but you didn't get back to me.'

'No, I'm sorry, I was out late giving a

lecture in Canterbury and didn't have time to check my messages until this morning. So what have you done with the necklace?'

'It's in my handbag,' she told him.

'What! Louise, that's foolhardy thing to have done! You could be in serious trouble for removing something valuable from the museum. Supposing it's part of their collection!'

'Then it won't be worth a light, will it?' she countered, disappointed by his response and suddenly feeling irrationally guilty. 'Anyway you removed the will.'

'That was hardly the same thing — not that I'm in a position to read it — let alone show it to the Dakars. Louise, if you were seen to remove that necklace . . . '

'But I wasn't, was I. Nigel said there's no CCTV in that gallery.' Which was just as well! Her cheeks burned as she remembered Nathaniel's kiss.

'I still think you were taking a risk. Whatever were you thinking of to bring it with you today? We'll have to phone Stuart Tomlinson and tell him what's happened — cover ourselves just in case.'

This was not the reaction Louise had anticipated, but she could see where Nathaniel was coming from. So great had been her delight in finding the necklace that the consequences of taking it back to Grace's hadn't really registered.

'Ok, you'd better phone him when we get to the nearest service station,' she said quietly, wishing she'd left the wretched necklace where it was.

'No, you'll phone him now!' Nathaniel commanded in an icy tone. 'Look Louise, surely you can understand that I don't want you implicated. You know what Ashley's capable of. Supposing he accuses you of stealing the necklace?'

'That's hardly likely, is it?' she said in a small voice. 'Ashley doesn't even know I've found it, and yes the thought had crossed my mind that — perhaps it isn't even the family heirloom that Marilena was given by Elinor Harper-Jones.'

'Ok, so let's get this phone call out of

the way. This is what I suggest you say . . . ' he told her brusquely.

Louise took her mobile from her handbag and, with trembling fingers, dialled the number from the address book in the glove compartment, as Nathaniel instructed, but it went to voice mail.

'Ask Stuart to phone me on my number as soon as he gets this message. Tell him it's urgent,' Nathaniel told her. When she had shut her phone and replaced it in her bag he said, 'Look, I've had an idea. We could get one jump ahead. We'll take the necklace to an antique shop in the famous Lanes. There's a guy I know who'd give us a reliable valuation. Then we'll know for sure what we're dealing with.'

As Nathaniel had predicted, his acquaintance, Stan, was prepared to take a look at the necklace then and there. The elderly man scrutinised it in silence for a few moments with his strong magnifying glass and then whistled.

'Who did you say this belonged to?'

'It's a family heirloom,' Nathaniel told

him. 'We're obviously going to have to insure it *if* — as you indicate — it's valuable.'

'Do you want me to do a proper valuation?' Stan asked. 'Of course — if you were interested in selling it to me then I'd give you a fair price, especially, as I suspect, it's got an interesting provenance. But, there again, you might prefer it to go to auction.'

'I'd have to get back to you on that after I've had a word with my — my grandmother,' Louise told him. 'It could be that she wants it to remain in the family.'

When Stan had completed the valuation, he wrote a figure on a piece of paper which was enough to make Louise's eyes water.

When they had left the shop Nathaniel said, 'Louise, have you ever thought about joining that amateur dramatics group that Ryan's sister belongs to?'

She stared at him. 'Amateur dramatics,' she repeated slowly. 'What on earth are you talking about, Nathaniel? Oh, I see . . . Well, surely you didn't expect me to tell that man how I'd really come by it, did you?'

He grinned and shook his head. 'Stan probably wouldn't have believed you anyway. Right now our main priority is to keep the darn thing safe.'

Suddenly he caught her to him in a tight embrace, almost taking her breath away.

'Nathaniel!'

'Quick, give me the necklace! Someone might be watching. I don't want anyone stealing your handbag.'

With great difficulty, she extracted the jewellery case from her bag and he placed it in his inside pocket. He then kissed her lightly on the mouth, leaving her tingling with anticipation.

'Sorry about that, but it was all I could think of in a hurry.'

'Now you've spoilt it,' she told him and he gave her an intense look, trying to work out if she was being serious. Her grey eyes met his dark brown ones steadily, and not for the first time he recognised the chemistry between them.

Louise's pulse had quickened and she wished the kiss had been for real. The touch of his lips on hers had done unimaginable things to her heart.

★   ★   ★

After lunch in a delightful restaurant Nathaniel knew, they went on a tour of the Royal Pavilion. Louise surveyed the onion-shaped domes and minarets with interest. It all seemed out of place amongst the rest of the town's buildings.

'It was designed by John Nash — you know — the architect of the Mall and Regent's Park in London,' Nathaniel informed Louise. 'It was built for the Prince Regent who later became King George IV, of course. He spent a lot of time in Brighton. Anyway, Nash got his ideas from India, which is why it looks rather like an Indian Maharajah's Palace.'

Louise gazed enchanted at the ceiling of the banqueting hall with its spectacular chandelier, complete with a silver dragon hanging by its claw. They then went into the Great Kitchen and admired the vast array of cooking utensils.

Afterwards, they walked along the promenade and found a café for tea. They talked about everything and anything.

'So does Brighton meet up to your expectations?' he asked her.

'More than — I love it. Thank you so much for bringing me here, Nathaniel.'

'You're welcome. I wanted to see some colour come back into those cheeks of yours. It's surprising what a bit of sea air can do to blow away the cobwebs.'

He caught her hand in his. 'So — are we friends again now?'

She nodded, her eyes shining.

'Good,' he slipped an arm about her waist, but didn't attempt to kiss her again.

As soon as they were back in the car, Nathaniel checked his mobile.

'Would you believe it — Stuart's sent me a couple of text messages! I was enjoying myself so much that I forgot to check. I'd better try to get back to him.

The sooner we get this sorted out the better!'

This time Stuart Tomlinson answered straight away.

'Stuart — Nathaniel here. I've got Louise Gresham with me and she's got a rather curious story to tell you.'

He handed the phone to Louise who tried to explain as best she could.

Stuart gasped. 'Louise, this is most irregular! Why on earth didn't you bring the necklace straight to me?'

'Because I thought it had to belong to Marilena Dakar. I'm sorry — I wasn't thinking straight.'

She looked helplessly at Nathaniel, who plucked his mobile from her fingers impatiently, and attempted to explain.

'This story is getting stranger by the minute,' Stuart commented when Nathaniel had passed the phone back to Louise. 'I gather Nat's got the item in his safekeeping now. Look Louise, I'll see you in my office at eight thirty sharp on Monday morning. If Nathaniel can join you, all well and good, and perhaps we should invite Mary Dakar along, too. As it happens, Julian Byrne, our jewellery expert, is dropping by to take a look at a gold torque, so that's providential. Now can I have another word with Nathaniel, please?'

'I was just keeping my fingers crossed that you wouldn't say anything about taking the necklace into that shop in the Lanes,' Nathaniel said when he'd finally finished the call.

'I'm not as stupid as I apparently look!' Louise said with spirit.

Nathaniel immediately looked contrite. 'Louise, I'm sorry. Look I'll juggle things round a bit and come with you on Monday morning. I'll also endeavour to see Philip and Mary before then. I didn't mention the copy of the will to Stuart. I'm itching to read it, but it's not for me to do that. It's got the name and address of Elinor's new solicitor stamped on it, so I can only assume it was drawn up and witnessed elsewhere just before Elinor died.

'Now; let's forget about all that for

the time being. I seem to remember you telling me Grace is out this evening, so would you care to dine with me? Unless, of course, you've got a prior engagement.'

'No, that is — yes, Nathaniel, I'd like that very much,' she stammered, her heart racing, 'although I'll need to change first.'

He surveyed her. 'You're absolutely fine as you are — actually, I meant a meal back at my place. Well, it's Matt's cottage really, but in his absence . . . '

'Oh, I see — that would be lovely.'

He laughed. 'Wait until you've eaten before you say that! Actually it's only cold chicken and stuff from the deli, and I'll cook some new potatoes.'

'Sounds wonderful.' She was aware that she was falling for the man sitting beside her, but knew she must hide her feelings.

★   ★   ★

The Victorian cottage in a picturesque village was a delight. Louise had tried to envisage where he lived when he stayed in the Whitchurch area, but this surpassed all expectations. He showed her where the downstairs cloakroom was and, after she'd freshened up, she found her way into a spacious sitting room with soft green walls and minimalist furniture — a chocolate brown leather suite, book lined walls and colourful rugs on a wood block floor.

Nathaniel handed her a glass of wine and the newspaper, and disappeared into the kitchen, whistling. In no time at all they were sitting down to their meal in the elegant dining room. The table was set to perfection with a sparkling white cloth and shining cutlery and glasses.

Louise had thought conversation might be difficult, but he made it easy for her by deliberately avoiding the subject of the necklace. She knew his passion was archaeology and he enthralled her with stories about various digs he'd been on. The time flew by.

For dessert they had fresh peaches accompanied by a delectable raspberry mousse topped with whipped cream, which he confessed he'd also bought.

They relaxed over coffee and mints, listening to hip-hop music. Suddenly, she caught sight of the clock and got to her feet.

'Nathaniel, it's been a lovely evening. More than I deserved after all the problems I've caused you. Thank you so much.'

He returned her gaze steadily and suddenly he had enfolded her in his arms and was kissing her as if he never meant to stop, tenderly at first but gradually becoming more passionate so that she felt engulfed in a maelstrom of emotions.

'Louise, I've been longing to kiss you properly,' he said softly against her hair. 'I realise it's unfair to Ryan but . . . '

She put a finger to his lips. 'Contrary to what you believe, I have no romantic feelings for Ryan. So far as I'm concerned we're just good friends.

Nathaniel removed the buckle confining her hair and it tumbled about her shoulders. He buried his face in it. 'Louise, I think I'm falling in love with you,' he murmured and it was as if all the sadness of the past months was washed away. She nestled in his arms feeling safe and secure, as if this was where she truly belonged.

The phone ringing broke the magic of the moment and brought them back to reality. Moving away from her, he picked it up.

'Olivia, I promised to ring, didn't I? Sorry, but I've been busy today. No, of course I haven't forgotten I'm expected for lunch tomorrow. I've been looking forward to it all week. See you soon — bye darling.'

All sorts of thoughts were flashing through Louise's mind as she listened unashamedly to this one sided conversation. She might have got over Ashley, and there had never been anything serious between her and Ryan, but what about Nathaniel? She knew that what she felt for him was different. His kisses had proved that, hadn't they?

Nathaniel had admitted that there had been other women in his life after Fleur, and that was hardly surprising. He was a good-looking man. But who was Olivia? Enough of a close friend for him to call her *darling*. Louise intended to tackle him, but somehow she couldn't bring herself to spoil the evening.

'Sorry about that, Louise. I ought to have checked my voicemail. It's getting to be a habit.'

'You shouldn't be so popular,' she rejoined lightly, fastening the buckle round her hair and trying to pretend she didn't care.

As he helped her into her jacket, his very closeness sent shivers dancing along her spine.

During the drive home, Nathaniel seemed rather preoccupied. Louise wondered if he was thinking of his visit to the unknown Olivia the following day.

'It's been a great evening, Nathaniel — in fact a great day altogether,' she told him as he pulled up outside Grace's.

'Good! I've enjoyed it too. We've had quite an adventure, haven't we? See you on Monday morning — bright and early.' And leaning across he kissed her gently on the cheek.

It was an anti-climax, Louise told herself, to what had indeed — until the last hour — been a great day. She blinked back the tears that were threatening to fall.

15

Louise arrived at the museum early on Monday morning, but not so early as Arlene who gave her a curious look and said, 'I don't know what you've been up to, Louise, but it must be serious if Mr Tomlinson wants to see you in his office first thing. It's also very inconvenient — as I'm under pressure to get that exhibition ready for the public — in case you've forgotten.'

Louise managed to look apologetic, but didn't attempt to enlighten Arlene as to what the meeting was about. She removed her jacket, tidied herself and went off to Stuart Tomlinson's office. Nathaniel was there already with Mary Dakar.

'This gets curiouser and curiouser,' Stuart Tomlinson said, as he studied the necklace on his desk. Now, I'm still not sure I've grasped the whole story so let's go through it again, Louise.'

Bit by bit the tale was told with Mary and Nathaniel chipping in from time to time. When Louise had finished, she felt like a criminal under investigation.

'It seems as if there are several issues here,' Stuart said, rubbing his chin and looking serious. 'Firstly how on earth are we to ascertain exactly who is the rightful owner? Before we discuss the matter any further, Mary, I'm going to ask Julian Byrne, our jewellery expert, to take a look. I've already put him in the picture, although I naturally haven't gone into details. He's come in early especially to give his valued opinion as to the authenticity of the necklace.'

Julian Byrne, an earnest-looking, middle-aged man with receding hair, peered intently through his special, jeweller's magnifying glass for several tense minutes, whilst the others waited expectantly. At last he looked up and cleared his throat.

'Obviously I'd need to make a more detailed examination and perhaps get a second opinion, but on first glance, this necklace seems to be of significant value,' he announced solemnly. 'The jewels are genuine and the setting quite exquisite. It's probably early eighteenth century. We could do with some provenance. I think we'll have to approach the Harper-Jones family in the first instance. Perhaps they've got some photographs of this particular piece of jewellery — either for insurance purposes or because it's part of a collection; unless of course — there's any record in your own archives?'

Stuart shook his head. 'Not that I'm aware of, no.'

'Oh, good heavens,' Mary sighed. 'Whatever am I going to say to Philip?'

'Nothing for the present,' Nathaniel told her. 'Mary you mentioned that you've got a copy of the letter Fleur had on her, from Ashley Harper-Jones' grandmother.'

'Oh, yes, I'd almost forgotten!' Mary produced the letter from her handbag and handed it to Stuart. 'The original is with our solicitor and he sent another copy to the Harper-Jones family. Perhaps this will make things a little clearer.'

Stuart perused it carefully. 'Hmm . . . This is such a complex matter, Mary — I'm wondering if you could have another word with your solicitor? If there are no records of this being museum property — or, at the very least, on permanent loan, then the decision as to who is the rightful owner will probably have to be resolved legally and, as you've said, in the absence of another will . . . '

Mary looked distressed and Louise put a comforting hand on her shoulder.

'If only that other will had turned up. This argument has raged on for years.'

Nathaniel suddenly unzipped his document case and with a flourish, produced the brown envelope. 'Maybe this should help to resolve the dispute. Again, thanks to Louise, we've managed to locate a copy of the new will at long last! Unfortunately, it must remain sealed, but — as you can see — it's got the name and address of Elinor's new solicitor stamped on the envelope!'

Stuart Tomlinson's eyebrows shot up. 'You two have certainly been busy; I suppose you haven't got any more surprises up your sleeves?'

They shook their heads and, for a moment, everyone seemed to have been dumbstruck, but then they all began talking at once.

Stuart raised his hands. 'Right. Thanks everyone. We're going to have to wait and see what Elinor Harper-Jones' solicitor has to say regarding the new will. Presumably it'll all depend on whether it's been signed and witnessed — to say nothing about the length of time that's elapsed.'

The meeting drew to a close and Stuart Tomlinson turned to Louise, his eyes full of sympathy. 'I realise you've been experiencing quite a difficult time recently, Louise. Nathaniel has explained to me what a shock you had when Ashley Harper-Jones turned up last week. I'm afraid I'd had no idea how traumatic everything's been for you until now. I suggest you take the rest of this morning off? Perhaps you could go with Mary to see her solicitor.'

Louise's cheeks coloured as she found herself the focus of attention.

'I'd like to of course,' she told him, but the new exhibition opens to the public at ten o'clock and Arlene needs me to . . . '

'Arlene has everything under control. Don't worry, I'll drop by and tell her you're needed elsewhere. I can stay around for a while if she needs my support — now off you go. Even if you can't get to speak with your solicitor today, Mary, you'll need to hand over the necklace. We can't risk it going missing again!'

'And don't worry about Philip. I'll stay with him until you get back,' Nathaniel said, seeing her concerned expression.

Mary expressed her gratitude and Nathaniel gave Louise an encouraging smile, making her heart race.

The visit to the Dakar's solicitor was productive but, unfortunately, there were no quick answers. He'd had a short space in between seeing clients and, as he was intrigued to hear that the necklace had turned up, had agreed to slot them in.

He contacted the firm in London who assured him they would check their records carefully and get back to him as soon as possible. Yes, Elinor Harper-Jones' name did ring a bell, but no, they didn't recall being informed that she'd died. After such a long time had elapsed it was unlikely that the will would hold much — if any weight. It was an extraordinary situation.

'Good heavens, it sounds as if we're in for a long wait,' Mary Dakar said worriedly as they sat over coffee before Louise returned to the museum.

'Oh, I'd like to think some good will come out of it to make it all worthwhile,' Louise said. She couldn't believe that all their efforts had been in vain. She thought of the time she'd spent with Nathaniel and those kisses. At least she had some memories to cherish.

★ ★ ★

Mary Dakar had given Louise permission to update Chloe with an edited account of what had been going on. Louise did this as she sat drinking coffee in her friend's pretty little garden.

'Wow! Trust me to miss all the excitement! Nothing like that ever happened when I was there!' Chloe exclaimed. 'So does the Dakar's solicitor think this necklace you've found *is* the one that was given to Fleur?'

'He's the very soul of discretion, but there's absolutely no record of it ever having been in the museum's collection.

'The Dakars must have been so shocked by Fleur's death it didn't occur to them the necklace was probably hidden in the museum. I suppose that's what Fleur must have been trying to convey to Philip.'

'So what will happen now?' Chloe asked, intrigued.

Louise shrugged. 'I'm afraid it's a waiting game. It all depends on what was written in the will. It's frustrating for the Dakars, but we'll just have to be patient. No doubt the Harper-Jones family will fight tooth and nail to keep the necklace, but there *is* a strong argument for it to go to Marilena. Anyway, that necklace is in safe custody now.'

Chloe nodded. 'It must have been a terrible shock when you discovered Fleur Dakar had also been engaged to Ashley Harper-Jones.'

Louise set down her coffee cup with a shaking hand. 'It was, but I'm just relieved I've had such a lucky escape. I mean — how *could* Ashley refuse to accept he's Marilena's father!'

'It doesn't bear thinking about, does it? So all that speculation about

Nathaniel Prentice was . . . '

'Just that — speculation!' It's a great pity some people don't have anything better to do with their time!' Louise said so sharply that Chloe gave her a curious look.

'Well, if it's any consolation, I for one didn't believe the gossip. Nathaniel's a lovely guy.'

Chloe got up to check on Ava who was fast asleep in her pram.

'I'm so lucky with Steve. He adores this little one. I don't know how I'll be able to part with her when it's time to return to work, but I have to admit I miss the buzz.'

She hesitated. 'What I have been wondering, Louise is . . . would you consider a job share?'

Louise's eyes widened. 'I'd love that Chloe, but I'm not sure how Arlene would view it.'

'She'll get used to the idea. Anyway, have a think about it . . . Now; changing the subject, do you know anything about knitting? I think I'm being too ambitious with this cardigan I'm trying to make for Ava. Mum isn't into knitting and I daren't ask my mother-in-law again!'

Chloe showed Louise the knitting which she'd got into an unbelievable tangle. They both dissolved into fits of laughter.

'Oh, I'm sure Grace would be only too pleased to help. She's brilliant with a pair of knitting needles,' Louise assured her friend, wiping her eyes.

After leaving Chloe's, Louise returned to work, feeling happier than she had done for a very long time.

⋆   ⋆   ⋆

After a busy morning at the museum on Thursday, Louise decided to take a stroll in the park opposite and purchase a takeaway sandwich and coffee in the café. She was just signing out when Nathaniel appeared from nowhere and, taking her arm, steered her out into the street.

'You and I need to finish that conversation we were in the middle of on Saturday when the phone rang.'

'Do we? I didn't think there was any more to be said,' she told him, attempting to shake off his arm.

'If we go through the park, there's a rather nice cafeteria on the other side of the lake,' he said, taking no notice of this remark.

'Yes, I know, I'm just going to buy some lunch there and have a picnic by the lake,' she said curtly.

'You're looking very serious, Louise. Is something the matter?' he asked as they crossed the road and went into the park.

'It depends what you mean by *the matter*. Everything seems to have ground to a halt and it's so frustrating. We can't do any more concerning the necklace because it's in the hands of the solicitors. Fortunately, Mr Tomlinson's been very understanding about it.'

'I think you know I'm not talking about the necklace, Louise.'

She gave him a searching glance, her heart hammering wildly. 'You're right — you see I've told you about Ashley and Ryan; but you've not been up front with me about your relationships, have you?'

He stared at her, trying to fathom out what she was getting at. 'How do you mean? You know about Fleur.'

'Yes, but that was years ago . . . I'm talking about *now*. What about Olivia? I mean — just what is she to you?' she demanded. 'One minute you're kissing me and the next you're calling Olivia, *darling*, and telling her how much you're looking forward to seeing her.'

To Louise's astonishment, Nathaniel burst out laughing. 'Oh, Louise — you've got totally the wrong end of the stick. Olivia is my eight year old niece. She's a little madam, but I love her to pieces.'

Louise felt very foolish, almost as foolish as when she'd mistaken Nathaniel for a stalker when they had first met.

'You know, I'm going to have to get used to your suspicious mind, aren't I?

You're always jumping to conclusions,' Nathaniel teased and took her in his arms.

She rested her head on his shoulder. 'That's because you're far too handsome to have been on your own all these years.'

He laughed. 'That's very flattering — I've already admitted there have been one or two other women in my life since Fleur, but no-one who's come into my heart in the way you have done,' he told her gently.

'So what about Arlene?'

'Arlene!' he exclaimed loudly, amber lights sparking dangerously in his eyes. 'No way! Louise, you have to believe me when I tell you that, from the moment she tried to discredit you in my eyes, I wanted no more to do with her. The photocopying incident was the final straw! Oh yes, I was fully aware of what she was up to on that occasion!

'I couldn't avoid taking her to my lecture in Canterbury last Friday, because it had been arranged way back, and it would have been churlish to have refused the invitation to lunch this Sunday, as it came from her elderly mother. Anyway, just between you and me, I think Arlene and Julian Byrne might be getting friendly. Julian's made a point of telling me he's asked her to accompany him to an exhibition in London.'

Their eyes met and he took her in his arms again and kissed her soundly.

'There — does that convince you that my feelings are for *you* and *you* alone?'

She nodded, her eyes shining with happiness. They bought their lunch and sat on a bench overlooking the lake where swans arched their graceful necks, and weeping willows dipped into the silvery water. It was a tranquil scene.

Nathaniel took her hands in his. 'Unfortunately, I don't have much free time for the rest of this week. Now, Mary doesn't want to leave Philip on his own for too long at the moment, so are you still good for the lecture at Marilena's school next Wednesday? I could really do with your support.' I know you're used to working with young people — and then afterwards, we'll be able to spend a bit of time with Marilena and Sophy.'

She smiled at him. 'Absolutely. I'd enjoy that. I'll look forward to seeing them again . . . There is something you could do for me in exchange,' she added tentatively.

He looked at her enquiringly.

'My parents are spending a couple of days in London at the end of next week, and then coming to Whitchurch on Sunday in time for lunch. It would be good if you could meet them.'

Nathaniel looked wary. 'But would they want to meet me? I mean wouldn't they give me the third degree after what happened between you and Ashley Harper-Jones?'

'They'll get used to you given time,' she said smiling.

He gave her a slight smile back. 'And what about you, Louise?'

'No, they're used to me already,' she

said, eyes sparkling with mischief.

For an answer he kissed her as if he never meant to stop. Any lingering doubts she might have had were washed away in a tide of joy.

★   ★   ★

To Louise's surprise, when she arrived home on Wednesday evening she found Mary waiting for her. A friend was visiting Philip so she'd felt able to leave him for a short while. The older woman could barely contain her excitement.

'Good news, Louise — and it's all down to you and Nathaniel. Our solicitor's been in touch. He's heard back about Elinor Harper-Jones' latest will. It's definitely in the strong room at the new solicitors' and they've verified it's been properly signed and sealed — so the copy you and Nathaniel found has to be bona fide.'

'Oh, that's fantastic,' Louise said, accepting the cup of tea Grace handed her.

'Not really — sadly the later will probably won't count for much after all this time. Apparently, there's a cut-off point. It's all rather complicated. The solicitor had absolutely no idea that Elinor had passed away. After she'd made the new will, he'd understood she was contacting her previous solicitor to ask him to return her original will, but he heard nothing further from her.'

Louise frowned. 'But I don't understand. You've just said there's some good news.'

'Wait — there's more. The necklace isn't part of the Harper-Jones' collection, after all. It's provenance was enclosed with the new will. It belonged to Elinor's family — the Barringtons. Her father gave it to her on her wedding day, so she was entitled to do exactly what she wanted with it. Copies of her letter were sent to the solicitor in York, as you know, in which Elinor made it clear she gave it to Fleur originally on her engagement to Ashley.

'Elinor stated that she wished Fleur

to keep the necklace after the engagement was broken off so that she had something for the baby which she firmly believed to be her grandchild.

Mary paused to sip her tea before continuing: 'The Harper-Jones' family solicitor retired recently and the new one, a Mr Duffield, is much more cooperative and on the ball. He's confirmed that *yes*, indeed there was such a letter predating Elinor's death. Elinor's original will has been kept on file because of the dispute regarding the necklace. Apparently, the only jewellery referred to in *that* will were the items that were part of the Harper-Jones collection — which the necklace you've discovered most definitely is not!'

Louise's eyes shone. Wow! That's wonderful news — so why did the Harper-Jones' believe it was a family heirloom?'

'It seems that there *is* a necklace missing from the collection. We'll probably never know what became of it, but I'm sure we can hazard a guess . . . '

'Ashley!' Louise and Grace exclaimed in unison.

'More than likely.' Miles Garret, Elinor's new solicitor, says that naturally Mr Duffield wants to see both the new will; together with the necklace and its provenance, to establish their authenticity. As Mr Garret has absolutely no intention of parting with any of these items, he's requested that either Mr Duffield or his representative from the York firm comes to London to view them, or else he will travel north himself in order to resolve the dispute.

'So it's now in the hands of three sets of solicitors and I suppose it'll take a long time to sort all the legal side out, but it's a start and very worthwhile.'

Mary hugged Louise. 'I just don't know how to thank you enough. It's taken such a weight off my mind.

'I'm only too pleased to be able to have found a way to repay a little of the kindness you and Dr Dakar have shown to me,' Louise told her huskily.

16

On Wednesday, Nathaniel's lecture, delivered to a group of sixth formers studying archaeology, went extremely well. Afterwards, Amelia Hardy invited Louise and Nathaniel to tea in her private sitting room, and Marilena and Sophy were allowed to join them.

As the girls went for a walk in the grounds with Louise and Nathaniel, he handed over a letter and parcel from Mary Dakar to her granddaughter.

Marilena scanned the letter eagerly. 'Grandma says Grandpa is 'heaps' better and he really likes my card.' Her face fell, 'But, she still doesn't think he'll be well enough to go to Crete this summer.'

She sounded so disappointed that Louise's heart went out to her.

'Oh, there'll be plenty of other years,' Nathaniel assured Marilena, slinging an arm about her shoulder.

'But, it was a promise. Grandpa said, '*When you're a teenager, I'll take you to Crete to see the villa where your mother stayed and to speak with some of the people who might remember her.*' And now I *am* a teenager, and I've still got to wait.'

Marilena looked tragic and Louise realised that life could be tough when you were only thirteen. Next year seemed light years away.

★   ★   ★

'Marilena's not going to let it rest, is she?' Nathaniel said, as they were driving away from the school. 'I'm going to have to talk to Mary about this fixation her granddaughter's got with Crete.'

'Oh, I'm sure once the holidays come and she's back in Whitchurch, she'll start thinking about other things.'

'Let's hope so. Thanks Louise for coming with me. We make a good team, don't we?'

'We certainly do. I almost forgot, Grace says to tell you she's made a huge ham and egg pie for supper and you're very welcome to share it.'

His eyes lit up. 'How can I refuse? Grace's pies are legendary. Everyone seems intent on fattening me up. They must think I look undernourished. You know that's something I haven't asked you — what are your culinary skills like, Louise?'

She looked at him startled, until she saw the twinkle in his eye. 'Passable, but I'm learning a lot from Grace. Of course, no-one makes a Yorkshire pudding like a Yorkshire woman. We're famous for it!'

He chuckled. 'Then it's a good job I like Yorkshire pudding! I suppose we could always have toad in the hole, followed by Yorkshire pudding and syrup for afters. I suppose you know that the way to a man's heart is through his stomach!'

When they pulled up outside Grace's house, Mary was there too, obviously waiting to hear all the news. A neighbour was staying with Philip. Nathaniel broached the subject of Crete, very tactfully.

'Ah, now I've had a piece of news which might just help solve that problem or at least help to soften the blow,' Mary told them, surprisingly unfazed. 'Sophy's obviously told her parents about our predicament. They're coming to England for a few weeks and, from here, going on a trip to Italy. They've emailed us to ask if Marilena would like to accompany Sophy. They think it would be good for Sophy to have a friend with her. So, what do you think?'

'I think that's a marvellous idea,' Nathaniel said sincerely.

'It would certainly take her mind off Crete,' Louise added.

Mary looked relieved. 'All being well, we'd take her there next Easter and she'll still only be thirteen.'

I think she's a very lucky girl to have so many people concerned about her welfare,' Grace said, as she served up the pie, 'Now, Nathaniel, has Louise asked you to Sunday lunch? Her parents are coming to stay for a couple of days.'

Nathaniel looked awkward. 'Yes — but I can't keep accepting your hospitality, Grace.'

Grace smiled. 'Nonsense — the more the merrier! It'll be on the table at one o'clock sharp.'

*   *   *

'I don't seem to see much of you nowadays,' Ryan grumbled as he encountered Louise in the cafeteria on Thursday lunchtime.

'Ah, well our paths haven't crossed recently so why don't we have a chat now?'

They collected their lunch and went to sit in a corner of the cafeteria.

'You'll be at a loose end when Nat's lectures have ended,' he commented, before biting into his sausage and bacon pasty.

'Oh, there's always plenty to do,' she assured him, knowing that he was right.

'So, where have you been hiding?' he

asked, reaching for his coffee.

'It was my day off yesterday.' Louise made her mind up, suddenly tired of all the subterfuge. 'Actually, I went to help Nathaniel with a lecture he was giving at Marilena Dakar's school in Sussex.'

Ryan raised his eyebrows. 'Then you must be a devil for punishment. Nathaniel's wedded to his work. He and Arlene make a fine pair. They'd be good for one another, but *you*, Louise — you don't want to find yourself in that sort of rut!'

'Thanks Ryan, I'll remember that,' she said, trying not to let him see how his words had affected her. She knew he wasn't right. Nathaniel could be great fun, and he'd assured her he wasn't involved with Arlene, so why did Ryan's remarks bother her?

'So how are things with you? How's your savings plan going?' she asked, desperate to change the subject.

He grinned. 'Oh, great thanks. I've bought myself three different coloured piggy banks and called them Dotty,

Lotty and Trotty,' he told her solemnly. 'Why are you laughing? I've labelled them outgoings, spending money and savings and, so far, I've only had to raid Trotty, the savings bank, twice! What about you?'

'Me? Oh, I put my spare cash in the building society . . . Oh, I see what you mean! I'm doing fine, thanks. Seriously, Ryan, if you were to put a little away in a savings account periodically, it'd soon mount up and, in the meantime, you'd earn a little bit of interest.'

Ryan snapped his fingers. 'I'm not silly Louise, I'm aware of savings accounts. Actually I've got a friend in the States who's asked me to visit her — so that's an incentive to save, isn't it?'

'Yes, of course it is.' Emily? Louise wondered with interest.

Just then Nathaniel appeared in the cafeteria and, as he made his way towards their table, Ryan got to his feet.

'Work beckons. So, remember what I've said, Louise. I'm a safe bet if you want to go out for a fun-filled evening.'

'Was it something I said?' Nathaniel enquired as Ryan dashed past him with barely a word.

'No — at least, I happened to mention that I'd assisted you with a lecture yesterday at Marilena's school.'

'I see.' Nathaniel gave her a searching glance. He'd obviously overheard Ryan's last remark. 'I thought you told me there was nothing going on between you and Ryan.'

'There certainly isn't so far as I'm concerned,' Louise told him indignantly.

'Are you absolutely sure about that? Because, from where I'm standing, things seem a bit different.'

'Nathaniel! How many more times do I have to tell you? We're just friends and colleagues — that's all. If you don't believe me, ask him!'

She downed the rest of her coffee and swept off, leaving him staring after her in bewilderment.

Louise spent the first part of the afternoon wondering if Nathaniel was

going to prove to be one of those possessive types who wouldn't let her speak to
another man. However, once she joined
him in the lecture room, he seemed his
normal self, and didn't refer to the incident until they had finished their tasks,
when he touched her arm and said,

'Sorry, Louise. I was in the wrong to
doubt you and I admit it!'

'We've got to learn to trust each
other,' she said huskily.

'You're absolutely right,' he said, and
pulling her to him, gave her a long
and satisfying kiss.

★   ★   ★

Louise's parents arrived around midday
on Sunday. Her father, in his late fifties,
hair greying at the temples, was still a
handsome man, whilst her mother was
an older edition of her daughter.

'You're in very good time for lunch,'
Grace told them, after the introductions
had been made. She declined Linda
Gresham's offer of help.

'Everything's under control. Louise is in charge of the Yorkshire puddings. There's no way I'm attempting that with a family from Yorkshire under my roof! Now, let me get you a coffee. I'm sure you could do with one.'

Linda Gresham came into the kitchen, as soon as she had freshened up and drunk her coffee, leaving her husband to read the Sunday paper.

'You're looking very well,' she told her daughter, 'and I think you've put on weight.'

'You can blame that on Grace's cooking,' Louise rejoined. 'So what have you been doing in London?'

'Go and have some catch-up time with your parents, Louise,' Grace ordered. 'Shoo! I'll give you a shout when I need you!'

*　*　*

Nathaniel arrived at exactly one o'clock, just as Louise had explained that some-one she'd become friendly with at the museum, who also happened to be a friend of Grace's, was joining them for lunch.

Linda Gresham looked at her daughter questioningly. 'Joanne told me that you were seeing someone else. Isn't it a bit soon, luv?'

'If you mean — is it on the rebound? Then no, it's most definitely not. Nathaniel's nothing like Ashley — you'll see.'

Her parents didn't look convinced, but Nathaniel was at his most charming and courteous and soon won the Greshams over. He'd come armed with flowers for Grace and a large box of luxurious petit fours for them all to share with their after dinner coffee.

Grace's roast beef was a triumph as usual, and Louise's Yorkshire pudding had turned out to perfection. Jim Gresham and Nathaniel established an immediate rapport, once they'd discovered they were both keen on tennis.

'I didn't know you played tennis, Nathaniel,' Louise said.

He looked amused. 'Well, there are still no end of things for us to discover about each other, aren't there? Until the other day, I didn't know you were good at making Yorkshire puddings!'

Louise and Nathaniel insisted on washing-up and making the coffee, leaving the others to chat.

'What delightful parents you've got, Louise,' Nathaniel said as they tackled the mountain of dishes.

'Yes, I know I'm fortunate to have such a lovely family. You'll be my father's friend for ever now he knows you're a tennis fan and you're *actually* been to Wimbledon! Wow!'

'Ah, well if that's all it takes to get him on my side! On a more serious note, Louise, do they know that you and I share some history?'

'Not yet. It's not an easy subject to bring up, because my father couldn't come to terms with what happened with me and Ashley and has shut it out of his mind.'

Nathaniel nodded. 'I can understand

that — *and* your mother?'

'On the surface she's sympathetic and very protective, but if ever I was to make the same mistake again . . . '

'Which is why I want you to be totally sure before we make a commitment.'

She gave him a shy smile. 'But you're *not* Ashley. I'm convinced you would never treat me like that.'

'And you're not Fleur. However much I cared for her, I suppose, deep down, I always recognised that there was a wild streak. I knew that she would never be satisfied with the sort of life I wanted.'

'And what makes you think I will?' Louise teased. 'Digging up old bones and relics — giving me endless pages of photocopying to do!'

For a moment a serious look crossed his face, but then — when he realised she was winding him up, he chuckled. 'You know I'd never try to make you give up your own interests for mine. You've got such a talent for arranging the exhibitions, and such a good knowledge of fine arts.'

He pulled her to him and she felt secure in his arms.

★   ★   ★

The next couple of days passed swiftly. Louise took her parents on a tour of the museum. To her astonishment, Arlene was generous in her praise of what Louise had contributed to the setting up of the displays and exhibitions throughout the museum.

'It's good to see you happily settled Lou,' her father said, as they strolled through the park afterwards.

'But, I could have wished you weren't so far away from us,' her mother remarked, wistfully.

'Well, we can't have everything, Linda,' her husband told her, 'and Louise's happiness must come first. I like that new young man of yours, Lou, but don't go rushing headlong into things this time round, will you, luv?'

Louise gave a little smile. She had told her parents about the recent incident with Ashley, and how Nathaniel had discovered they'd both suffered at the hands of the same man.

'Nathaniel would never treat me like that, Dad,' she told him. 'Anyway, I've grown up a lot since then. I'm just glad Nathaniel was waiting for me round the corner.

Her parents exchanged glances. They could have wished their daughter had met Nathaniel first. It would have saved her such a lot of heartache, but they knew that the experience with Ashley had made her more mature and a much stronger character.

All too soon, Louise was saying goodbye to her parents with a promise to visit them as soon as she got some holiday.

*   *   *

That Sunday was one of the happiest Louise had ever known. Nathaniel took her to Lullingstone Roman Villa, situated in the Darent Valley, in some of the prettiest Kent countryside she had seen so far.

'This villa is one of England's most important archaeological sites,' Nathaniel reminded her as they wandered round. He was in his element as he pointed out the mosaic floors depicting mythological characters; the bathing suite and the wall paintings.

Louise was enthralled by the items displayed in the exhibition, many of them excavated in the 1950s. She was amazed to discover there was even evidence of there having been an early Christian chapel on the site.

They had a leisurely lunch at Farningham, another Kentish gem with its weather boarded mill and thirteenth century church.

'Kent's full of surprises,' Louise said as they sat over coffee.

Nathaniel smiled at her. 'There's certainly a lot to see and do in this area. Another time I'll take you to Lullingstone Castle. It's renowned for its *World Garden* with plants from all over the globe. Now, how d'you fancy having a stroll by the river at Eynesford?'

'That sounds wonderful. I need a walk after this lovely meal.'

'So, have you enjoyed the day?' Nathaniel asked, as they strolled along by the river, hand in hand.

'Every minute,' she assured him, eyes sparkling. 'Thank you for showing me this lovely place, Nathaniel.'

'Nat,' he corrected gently.

They had reached a wider part of the river bank. It was cool and shady and the trees formed a green canopy. Slipping an arm about her waist he drew her to him.

'I've fallen in love with you, dearest Louise,' he told her softly, before his lips met hers.

In between kisses he asked, 'Do you think, given time, you might come to love me too?'

A surge of happiness swept over her, her grey eyes shone. Her heart was pounding so hard that she felt sure he must feel it. She met his dark brown eyes with their dancing amber lights, and saw the love in them.

'Just give me a couple of minutes to get used to the idea,' she said and reaching up entwined her arms around his neck and kissed him again, in a way that told him all he needed to know.

We do hope that you have enjoyed reading this large print book.

Did you know that all of our titles are available for purchase?

We publish a wide range of high quality large print books including:
Romances, Mysteries, Classics
General Fiction
Non Fiction and Westerns

Special interest titles available in large print are:
The Little Oxford Dictionary
Music Book, Song Book
Hymn Book, Service Book

Also available from us courtesy of Oxford University Press:
Young Readers' Dictionary
(large print edition)
Young Readers' Thesaurus
(large print edition)

For further information or a free brochure, please contact us at:
Ulverscroft Large Print Books Ltd.,
The Green, Bradgate Road, Anstey,
Leicester, LE7 7FU, England.
Tel: (00 44) 0116 236 4325
Fax: (00 44) 0116 234 0205

Other titles in the
Linford Romance Library:

THE SECRET FRIEND

Valerie Holmes

Sophia has a secret friend, James Dalesman, her soul mate. In their youth, the two pledged that no one would ever come between them. Ten years later, Sophia is an heiress to a wealthy estate and must provide a respectable heir to carry on the family's wealth; while no matter what James has done, his position has never been equal to hers. Can Sophia's father, society's rules, or even a war tear the couple apart, or is it their destiny to be together despite the obstacles in their way?